MINE FOR THE HOLIDAYS

a BBW Holiday Romance

MEGAN WADE

Copyright © 2020 by Megan Wade

All rights reserved.

No part of this book may be reproduced in any form or by any electronic or mechanical means, including information storage and retrieval systems, without written permission from the author, except for the use of brief quotations in a book review.

editing: More Than Words

❀ Created with Vellum

DELANEY

"Mom. Hey, can I call you back?" I say, trying to juggle my phone and packing material. "I'm just in the middle of—"

"This won't take long," my mother's deep and croaky voice insists down the line. She sounds like she spent her entire adult life sucking down a pack a day, but she's never smoked a cigarette in her life.

"OK, Mom," I say, as I tuck my cell between my shoulder and my ear so I can continue packing orders of my custom skincare range. My business is finally getting off the ground after five years of refining my formula, not to mention the years of college and learning the business before that. Success has been a long hard road, but I've been lucky to have my best friend, Liz, by my side the whole time. She stands across from me now, smiling to herself because she knows how overbearing my family can be. I mean, they *mean* well, but there's a reason I moved to San Francisco to set up shop.

"As you know, the holidays are coming," Mom says as I make noises to show her I'm listening.

"Uh-huh, Uh-huh."

"And as always, we're doing Thanksgiving at your aunt's house—you're coming, I'm sure."

"About that, Mom. There's a chance I won't make it. I'm kinda swamped with—"

"Nonsense. You'll be here, and you'll bring that boy you've been talking about with you. The entire family is *dying* to meet him. We've got an extra place setting just for him. Guest of honor!"

"Ahhhh." My brain returns the 'station closed' signal as I try to figure a way around this one.

In their constant efforts to see their only daughter 'happy and settled before she's too old to have children,' my mom and great-aunt tried setting me up with 'nice boys' they felt were suitable for a 'girl like me'—a girl like me being a thirty-six-year-old non-starter with bright red hair and more than my fair share of curves. They've set me up with the son of a business associate, a college professor seeking tenure at the state's smallest college, a bank manager, and a flight attendant Mom met on their trip to Hawaii last year. And do you know what all these men had in common? They wore glasses—thick glasses. If this doesn't tell me something about my attractiveness level, then I don't know how to take it.

Now, my family has never put me down about my looks, but they've certainly never called me pretty either. And that's OK. I know I'm nothing special to look at. And I also know that this is their misguided attempt to help me find the happiness they've all enjoyed in their lives. Mom and Dad were high school sweethearts who have been devoted to each other since day dot. And my big brothers all found their One before they even finished college. So that just leaves me. The youngest, and the hardest to love. I know I'm affecting their picture-perfect bubble with my constant singleness. So to save myself from further humiliation being set up with someone I have zero chemistry with, this year I told them I was already seeing someone—an imaginary someone, but someone who'll keep the matchmaking at bay. At least, that was the plan, anyway.

"He *is* coming, isn't he?" Mom asks, and I wonder *why* I didn't expect this. *Of course they want me to bring him to Thanksgiving.* "Because you know your Aunty Joan won't be with us much longer. Her dying wish is to see you happy. You can't let her go thinking she has unfinished business."

I press my fingers to the bridge of my nose

and wince. *I can't believe she's using my great aunt against me.* Aunty Joan is the only other single woman in the Gilchrist family. She's my late grandmother's older sister and is the most lovely woman you've ever met. But she has regrets—lots of them. And one of her biggest worries is that I'll end up lonely and childless like her. And God help me, I can never say no to her.

"Sure, Mom," I say, closing my eyes against the lie that's about to come out of my mouth. "Liam will be there. He's...uh...*really* looking forward to it." When I open my eyes, Liz has frozen in place, her brow raised in a silent, *how are you going to pull that off?*

"Brilliant!" Mom says, glee coating her voice. "Because Aunty Joan also has a surprise for us all. I'm not supposed to tell you, but I know you and Liam will need to clear your schedules, so you have to promise me you'll both act surprised on the day."

"Surprised?" Panic grips my chest as I lock eyes with Liz as she silently asks me what's going on. "By what, Mom?"

"By the tickets. Aunty Joan wants us all to go on one last family vacation together. So she's surprising everyone with an all-expenses-paid holiday cruise. Isn't that wonderful?"

"But... But... What about work? What if we can't get away?"

"Well, that's why I've warned you. So you can organize to have Liz look after things for you for ten days. And Liam needs to come. She bought a ticket for him too. It's all nonrefundable, and I don't need to tell you how important it is to keep Aunty Joan happy." I should probably mention that my aunt is incredibly wealthy. She's also very generous, and my family back home enjoy a lot of perks due to that generosity. They constantly worry about rocking the boat and falling out of favor—another reason I left Oakwood Falls to strike out on my own—and I don't think any less of them for it, it just isn't something I'm comfortable with. I have an intense need to do everything in life on my own terms. Call me crazy, call me hard-way Delaney, but it's just how I roll. And I'm happy that way.

"Mom—"

"I know. I'm asking a lot. But she's old, and she doesn't think she has another Christmas in her. We have to do this for her. As a *family*." In other words, '*Don't be difficult, Delaney.*'

A small squeak comes out of my mouth that sounds a lot like, "OK."

"Wonderful," Mom says, breathing a sigh of relief. "And tell that boy of yours we can't wait to see him in the flesh. He's made an old woman very happy."

"OK, Mom," I say, but it's more of a whisper

because I can barely breathe anymore. What the hell kind of hole have I dug myself into? This was supposed to be a little white lie, designed to make everyone happy, and keep me from feeling uncomfortable. I could have gone to Thanksgiving alone and said there was a dental emergency—I told them Liam is a dentist—and he couldn't come. But now there's a cruise and nonrefundable tickets, and everyone is counting on me to produce a boyfriend that doesn't exist. *Oh, God, what have I done?*

As I disconnect the call, I drop my weight in the nearest chair and let out a self-pitying sob. "I'm going to hell!"

"Oh, honey, it can't be that bad," Liz says, stopping what she's doing and crouching down in front of me. "So you made up a fake boyfriend and they want to meet him. We've all been there at some point in our lives."

Shaking my head, I take a deep, steadying breath. "You don't understand. It's not that they want to meet him, it's that they bought *us tickets* to go on a *family cruise*."

Liz's eyes bug out. "They did what?"

I relay the rest of the conversation to her, explaining how adorable Aunty Joan is and that she's so excited about my relationship with the fictional Liam that she's booked and paid for a family cruise. "How am I gonna tell them I *lied?*

She's so old! The disappointment itself could kill her! And I don't want to be the person who sent a sweet old lady to her grave. Oh, God," I wail. "What the hell was I thinking?"

"It's OK," Liz consoles. "We'll figure this out."

"How?" I ask, seriously close to tears. "I don't know any dentists named Liam, do you?"

"No. But maybe we could find one?"

"Are you for real?" I laugh at the absurdity. "What do I do, put a want ad in the paper that says 'Single Woman Seeks A Dentist Named Liam For The Holidays'? I imagine that'll solve all my problems in a jiffy."

"Well...it'd be a start, right? But I'm not thinking the want ads as much as I'm thinking an escort. You know, like that movie 'The Wedding Date'. You could totally pull off Debra Messing in her heyday."

"I'm two to three times the width of Debra Messing."

She waves a hand dismissively. "Tomayto – tomarto. What we really need is to find your Dermot Mulroney. Some guy who's super hot and will show everyone that Delaney Gilchrist is *not* some charity case who has to beg for dates."

I bark out a laugh. "You're right. I'm such a loser that I have to *pay* for one."

"So? Better than killing your great aunt, right?

And, *ohmigosh!* I just thought of the perfect guy for this!"

"What? Who?"

"My brother's college roommate is in town. He just came back here after spending half his life chasing an acting career in LA."

"An actor?"

"Yes! It's like the gods are working in your favor. He's down on his luck right now—he's actually been staying in Burt's guestroom for the last couple of weeks. And I think Burt would be more than happy to have his house back, and Nate could do with the cash to help him get back on his feet."

"This isn't currently convincing me."

"No. No! Nate's a great guy. It's just my sister-in-law isn't too keen on sharing her space, and you know how Burt can't say no to a friend in need. So you'll be doing everyone a favor while helping yourself, and just between you and me, Nate is *hot.* Think Jax Teller in Sons of Anarchy vibe, but with the body of Chris Hemsworth."

"Jeez. *Now* you're selling it to me," I say, feeling a little more positive about this plan of action. "Do you really think he'd do it?"

"Well, you're paying him to go on an all-expenses-paid cruise, I think most humans would jump at the chance. Should I call him?" She pulls her cell from her pocket and holds it out.

Blowing out a slow breath, I try to think of any other way I could get out of this cruise without admitting I'm a liar, upsetting my entire family, *and* hurting my aunt in the process. When I draw a blank, I simply shrug. "Why not? It can't hurt to at least *talk* to the guy, right?"

"Exactly! I'll set it up right away."

NATE

I step into the coffee shop and look around, the sound of happy chatter filling my ears while the scent of coffee and baked goods hit my nose. It's an all too familiar scene. I spent more time running a coffee house than I did on set during my early years in LA. And even when I started working small parts enough to ditch the barista life, I never lost the feeling that I was only one step away from being right back inside one. And I suppose I was right. Fifteen years of striving yet never achieving and here I am, in a coffee shop for a role of a different kind. I wouldn't call LA the place where dreams go to die, but it won't be remembered as my happy place either. San Francisco on the other hand, has always felt like home. And it's where I'll make a new beginning. I just need to find some direction first...

"Nate?" A small hand gently taps me on the shoulder, and I'm quick to turn around. Liz told me to look for a woman with red hair. But when my heart starts galloping in my chest, I realize this is more than a woman. What I'm confronted with is a curvy goddess.

Despite the nerves that clearly define her features, her sapphire-blue eyes shine like the gems they are, set in a heart-shaped face with bright pink lips and straight white teeth. Her skin looks so smooth that I immediately want to reach out and run the edge of my thumb along her cheekbone. And her hair...well, it isn't just *red*. It's a mix of auburn and copper, and it hangs in elegant waves over one shoulder, leaving the other exposed. If I was a vampire, I'd want to lean in and take a bite. Hell, I'm nowhere near being a vampire, and still I wouldn't mind leaning in and biting the soft flesh in the curve of her neck. If the coffee wasn't overpowering everything else in the room, I imagine she'd smell like frangipani and vanilla, or water lilies and apples. Something fragrant yet sweet to go with her timeless curves and lush-looking body. *Liz has been holding out on me.*

"You must be Delaney," I say, a slow smile curving my lips as my eyes take a slow trek down her fuchsia-colored dress. It hugs her curves and shows me exactly where I'd like to grab onto as I drive myself inside her. *Whoa. Calm down. She's not yours...yet.*

"I am." Delaney smiles in return then gestures to a free table. "Should we sit?"

"Sure."

She keeps her spine straight as she settles across from me, immediately reaching into her bag and pulling out a cream-colored folder. "I already took the liberty of ordering coffee for us," she says, her hands resting on top of the folder. "And I've compiled a list of information you'll need to complete this job, as well as the remuneration package I'm willing to offer you for the time spent playing this character for me—if you choose to do it, of course." *I'd like to do you...*

She keeps staring at me and I realize she's probably waiting for me to say something.

"Ah, sure." I knit my brow slightly. *She's straight to business. OK. I can work with that.* "Do you think I could get a look at that?"

For a moment, she seems like she doesn't know what I'm talking about. "Oh!" All at once she lifts her hands and pushes the folder across the table to me. "Sorry. This isn't something I do all that often. I'm a little flustered if that isn't evident."

"I wouldn't have known if you didn't tell me,"

I say, giving her a wink as I lift the cover of the folder open and peer inside. When she pulls her hand back to her side of the table, she takes the sugar dispenser with her, granulated crystals spilling everywhere.

"Shoot!" She moves frantically to try and scoop up her mess, and I'm quick to help and attempt to put her at ease.

"Hey," I say, covering her hand with mine. "How about we try and relax a little? From what Liz told me, it seems like you've got a lot of pressure on you right now, and all you're doing here is interviewing for some help."

"I suppose you could look at it like that," she says, pulling her hand away as the blush creeps from her cheeks down her chest. She's adorable.

"OK. So let's treat this like any other interview. Pretend you're hiring me to work in your company. You work in skincare, right?"

"Right." She smiles, and already I can see her start to relax as a waitress brings us our coffees then helps clean up the sugar from the table. I have a handful of facts available to me about Delaney since Liz is my best friend's sister. In the few weeks I've been back in town, she's told me enough about her job for me to know that Delaney is the brains behind a successful skincare range that's only now finding its feet. On top of that, I know that Delaney's family has been pressuring her to settle down and marry which is why she's looking to hire a stand-in boyfriend to get them off her back.

"What would you ask someone you were interviewing for a position in sales or customer service?" I put it that way since really, that's exactly what she's hiring me for. It's just that the customers are her family, and the product I'm selling is our fake relationship—not that that part is going to be particularly hard. If I'd met her under any other circumstance, I'd be dating her for free. But as it is, this is a business arrangement organized to make her life easier. From what Liz said, she doesn't want a man in her life. Her business is her baby and that's the way it's going to stay, and I can respect that. It doesn't stop me from wanting her, but I respect it. And quite frankly I need the cash. So, I tuck my basal reaction to her deep down inside and get into character mode. I didn't spend all those years honing my acting skills for nothing.

"I'd ask what made you feel you're right for the position and my company." She blushes slightly as she lifts her mug to her lips and takes a sip. *God, she's sexy.*

"OK. Would you like me to answer as me, Nate Charmers? Or as..." I pause as I open the folder and do a quick scan of the character sheet. "Liam Tribbiani. A dentist from Minnesota?"

"Um, both?" She grimaces a little as she laughs. I realize it's my new favorite sound.

"OK. Well, as myself, I am a good fit because I've studied acting for most of my life, had a handful of supporting roles in both TV and film. And while I never became a shining star, I also didn't receive many complaints. I'm good at what I do, and you'll see that in how easily I slip into the character of Liam Tribbiani."

"What made you quit?"

"Acting?" She nods. "A long line of things, really. It's a hard industry—all entertainment is—and I realized that staying in LA, chasing after something that was never going to happen, was slowly chipping away at my self-esteem. Things in my life changed. It was just time."

"That makes sense. I can't imagine it's easy dealing with the constant auditions and rejections. I'm impressed you stayed there so long."

"I'm nothing if not tenacious."

"That's a point in your favor."

"Good to know," I say, grinning at her as we lock eyes and I take a sip of my coffee.

"OK, so now be Liam. I'd like to...meet him." She giggles a little as she cradles her mug against the table. "This feels crazy," she whispers. "I don't know how I let Liz talk me into it."

"It's not crazy. You'd be amazed how many

people hire actors to stand in for people in real-life situations."

"So you've done something like this before?"

"Pretended to be someone's boyfriend?"

"Yes."

"I have. A few times, actually. Not on this scale. But I have played the dutiful boyfriend or husband role more than once."

"Strangely, that makes me feel a hell of a lot better. OK, so be Liam."

"Show me your teeth." She gives me an over-exaggerated smile. "Hmm. I can see you've got a slight rotation of the lower right canine that I'm happy to fix for you the next time you visit my office."

She laughs and sits back in her seat as she meets my eyes. "Do you really think you can pull this off? I mean, you have to pretend to be into me for a solid month. We get a test run at Thanksgiving, but that's only one day and night. We can meet in between to make sure we have our story ironed out, but once we get on that cruise ship, we'll be stuck with each other for a whole ten days. There won't be any hiding. Although, if you get tired of me, I suppose we can feign a fight or something..."

"I won't have an issue pretending to want you, Delaney. I assure you."

"OK." She worries her lips together as she

sucks a deep breath in through her nose, seeming to completely miss the compliment I just paid her. *Did I mention she's adorable?* "Then I guess...I guess you're hired."

"I won't let you down," I say, holding my hand out to shake hers across the table. The moment she places her delicate paw inside the meaty hand that is mine, a brand-new blush creeps over her cheeks. "That's something you'll have to work on."

"What is?" she asks.

"Blushing every time I touch you."

She licks her lips. "How do I do that?"

"Well, you expect that I'm always going to touch you. And I will, Delaney, a lot. Liam is a hands-on kind of guy." I lean in and give her a wink before pressing a soft kiss to the top of her hand. I swear her face catches fire. *I think this job is going to be the best one I've ever had.*

DELANEY

"Tell me this isn't dumb. Tell me I'm nervous for nothing. Or better yet, tell me to cancel the whole thing," I say into my cell as I roll a straightening iron through my hair to create the perfect beach waves. Liz is on the other end of the line offering me moral support while I quietly—scratch that, I *very noisily* freak out. *Why did I think I could go through with this?*

"Del, you're going to be fine," Liz assures me, laughing at the way I'm huffing and puffing and finding a thousand reasons why I can't even go to Thanksgiving dinner anymore. I've contemplated calling to tell my mother I have food poisoning, that there was an emergency at work, that I was kidnapped and being held for ransom until *after* the holidays—I even entertained the idea of saying I have a case of the bubonic plague. All options seeming better than going through with this ridiculous farce.

I know I should just call it off and come clean, but that would truly be worse than all my pretend excuses put together. Not only will my entire family be disappointed in me, but they'll feel sad and sorry for me too. I'm the girl who can't get a boyfriend. I'm the girl who needs my family to set her up. I'm the girl who had to *pay* a boy to *pretend* to like her... See where I'm going with this?

"I just hate lying. I mean, I know everyone lies a little to their parents to keep them off their backs. But this one is a doozy."

"It's for a good cause though. Your Aunty Joan will be so happy seeing you coupled up, and you won't be forced to sit next to another glasses-wearing stranger that makes your skin crawl. Nate is the kind of man your family should have been setting you up with all along. He's gorgeous to look at, and besides the good looks, he really is a great guy—even when he *isn't* playing a part. He'll look after you, I promise."

Switching the phone to speaker, I let out a sigh as I place it on the bathroom counter before I move to the other side of my hair. "He makes me nervous," I admit.

"Nate?" Liz laughs. "He's like, a giant teddy bear squish ball, Del. There's nothing to be nervous about. Did I tell you he took me to an awards dinner once? It was back when I was cheerleading, and there was this big—"

"Wait. You were a *cheerleader?*" I ask, feeling blindsided since I *never* took Liz as the cheerleading type. We met in college and she was always kinda...optimistic emo—if that could ever be a thing. She loved nineties grunge rock and oversized sweaters and smoky eyeliner and nude lips. I couldn't imagine her being all glittery and...peppy.

"I haven't told you? Gosh. It was all I cared about in high school, but then I broke my ankle at the start of senior year and never went back to it. Blessing in disguise, really, because like I was telling you, there was this awards night *no one* told me about. So, I didn't have a date, and I was faced with either going stag and looking like a loser, or finding a date at the last minute. Mom suggested I go with my brother or my cousin, but that would just be social suicide, and since Nate was over at the time, he said he'd do it. Perfect gentleman the whole time, really easy-going. You seriously couldn't ask for a better fake boyfriend."

"So, this is something he's done a lot then? Rescue desperate women from the judgmental stares of others?"

"I guess you could say that," she says with a laugh. "It's not an advertised service though."

"Is working as an escort something people *can* advertise?"

"I don't know that he'd label himself as an escort," she says. "He's more like a knight in shining armor, I guess. So don't go thinking he sells his body to the night." She says the last part like she's a vampire on Sesame Street, and I can't help but laugh.

"OK. Note to self: don't treat Nate like a hooker—"

"Except if *he* comes onto *you*. Paid or not, if that man tried to take me to bed, I'd throw down like a five-dollar hooker on Taco Tuesday."

"*That's five tacos for one blowjob! har har har!*" I say, mimicking The Count before Liz and I both fall into fits of giggles.

"He could charge me a dollar per thrust and I'd happily pay up," she says between snorts.

"*One thrust! Two thrusts! Three and four! Five thrusts, six thrusts! Ten thrusts more!*" I continue counting and rhyming while I finish with my hair and switch off the flat iron. Liz is in a fit of giggles in my ear, so of course I keep going, getting dirtier and dirtier as I move through my apartment, collecting my things before I head out to pick Nate up and drive out to my parents'. "*Oh! Yes! That's great thrusting! Har har har!*" Just as I finish my final Count von Count cackle, I pull my door open and find myself face to face with the delicious Nate himself. His hand is raised as if ready to knock, and he has a highly amused smirk on his face. "Liz, I have to go." I hang up before she can even respond then look up to Nate's mirthful blue eyes. "Don't you just love Sesame Street?" I give him my best impression of Julia Roberts in Pretty Woman.

His grin grows wider, but he doesn't miss a beat. "More than life itself," he says, stepping to the side so I can lock up.

"I thought *I* was coming to collect *you?*" I say, gathering my wits as I try to balance a pumpkin pie and my overnight bag while I lock the deadbolt. Nate takes the pie and bag from me. "Thank you."

"No problem," he says, sneaking a look under the bakery box's lid. "And I figure Liam is the kind of boyfriend who would drive his girlfriend all the way to Oakwood Falls. So, I'm here to pick *you* up. You look gorgeous, by the way." His eyes travel from my carefully made-up face and hair to my heeled feet. My heart hammers in my ears.

"Ah, thanks," I say, smoothing my hand over the forest green dress I'm wearing, I suck my stomach in a little harder as I meet his eyes. "You look really handsome too." Not that he needs to put much effort in. He's naturally stunning—broad shoulders, muscular frame, and square jaw. When Liz said he was a cross between Jax Teller and Chris Hemsworth, she wasn't half wrong. When I first met him in the coffee shop, he was wearing a white T-shirt and jeans. Just the sight of him almost got me pregnant. Today he's wearing charcoal slacks, a button-up shirt, and a pale blue tie. His shoulder-length hair is pulled back at the nape of his neck, and the stubbled jaw he was sporting a few days ago is now shaved clean. He smells like the woods with a dash of spice and orange. And everything about him is so perfect that this time I think I'm pregnant with twins. Someone needs to make protective glasses for these kinds of situations because my ovaries ache from looking at him.

"Liam Tribbiani. At your service." He gives me a slight bow.

"Getting into character already, huh?" I flash him a grin as I drop my keys and phone in my purse then reach for the bakery box.

He moves it out of my reach. "Liam does all the heavy lifting," he says, giving me a wink.

"Does Liam always talk in third person too?" I ask, heading for the elevator and hitting the call button.

"He can if you want him to," Nate says, hanging back as the doors open and I step inside. He follows me in and hits the button for the lobby. It's all so fluid and natural that I honestly forget for a moment that this is all just an act. Liz did say he's a good actor, and after our conversation just now, I'm wondering what else he's good at too...

"I don't," I say, sneaking a glance at this hunk of a man and finding him smiling my way. "Something amusing?"

He inhales before he shakes his head. "I'm just surprised is all."

"About?"

"Why a woman as beautiful as you would need a guy like me." His eyes dance and my face heats. The comment is confronting and flattering all at the same time, and I'm having trouble figuring out if he's serious or if it's just part of the act.

"Maybe tone down the flirting a bit," I say, erring on the side of caution so I don't get too carried away here. Being so close to a man as beautiful and charming as Nate is nerve-wracking enough without complicating things by convincing myself his kindness is actual interest. I need to remember that this is a boss/employee situation in order to keep my head clear. We're both playing a part. Nothing more. "We've been dating six months already, so you really don't need to use any lines on me. To Liam, I'm a sure thing, and he'd probably be getting bored with me by now."

Nate's brow knits before he inhales and opens his mouth, about to say something. But the dinging of the elevator arriving on the ground floor cuts him off. "After you," he says instead, gesturing for me to go ahead of him.

We walk to his car in silence, but when he opens the sedan's passenger door to let me in, he pauses before he closes it.

"You're wrong," he says, resting an elbow on the top of the navy-blue door.

"About?"

His eyes lock on mine as he waits a beat before he answers. "Liam," he says finally. "He wouldn't be bored." And with that, he closes the door and heads around to the driver's side. Leaving me trying to work out what the hell he meant by that. I mean, a guy like him couldn't possibly like *me*. Surely he's just being nice and all these compliments mean nothing. This is just part of the service... *Right?*

NATE

"Why a dentist?" I've loosened my tie slightly, trying to be a little more comfortable in this monkey suit for the journey. Normally, I'm a sweats and T-shirt kind of guy. I only bought my first suit because my grandfather insisted that every man needs at least one good suit in their wardrobe. Since then, there have been times when life or the job has required it. So as much as I hate wearing them, I have a couple for special occasions... Like pretending to be someone's long-term boyfriend, for example.

"Oh, gosh. You're going to think I'm really silly when I tell you," Delaney says, glancing at me. She's kept her eyes firmly out the window throughout most of the first hour of our journey. I don't know if she's too nervous to look at me, or if she just doesn't like what she sees. I've been told in the past that I'm a decent looking guy, but I also know that you can't please everyone. Spending a large portion of your life being told you don't have the right look for a part will hammer that one home pretty fast, so I don't pretend to think I'm anything particularly special.

"Try me," I say, flashing her a smile when our eyes meet for the briefest of moments.

"Well, this all started after the last time my mother set me up on a date. The man had zero personality and I kind of think he was a little bit cross-eyed. At least, one of his eyes seemed to turn toward his nose more often than it was looking at me. Maybe that's a lazy eye or something? Or maybe he found me eye-rollingly painful to be around. I don't know. But, I felt that I had done my daughterly duty, entertaining the idea of these men for the sake of my well-meaning mother and aunt. So when Mom called and mentioned she met *another* 'nice young man', I told her that I was already seeing someone. Which is where the lie begins."

"Let me guess, you were sitting at the dentist during this phone call?" I ask.

"The subway actually. I told her I was seeing someone. And she asked who. I wasn't really prepared for the lie, so I was looking around at all the little advertisements they have up on the walls, and there was a movie poster with Liam

Neeson in it. So that's where I got Liam from. Then the person sitting next to me was wearing one of those shirts that say, 'it's a moo point.' You know that line from Friends when Joey says it's a moo point because a cow's opinion doesn't actually matter?"

"It's all moo," I say, smiling because I'm thoroughly entertained by how her mind has pieced this all together.

"Right. Well, I looked at her shirt and I thought 'Joey Tribianni'. Which is how Liam got his last name. Then of course, there was an ad about teeth whitening above the seat across from me, so that's how he became a dentist. It's not the most inventive of stories, but I didn't really think I was ever going to have to produce the man. I hoped I'd be able to make up an excuse for Thanksgiving then say we broke up before Christmas then be very sad over New Years, and just be *left alone* these holidays. But then my aunt —who thinks she isn't going to live to see another holiday—went and bought all these tickets for a family cruise and well, you know the rest."

I take my eyes off the road for a second to glance her way. "For what it's worth, I get it," I say.

"You do?"

"Hell, yeah." The leather on the steering wheel creaks as I grip it a little too hard, trying to find the right words here. "I'm not trying to talk shit about your family, I'm really not. But they should probably learn to back off and let you live your life the way you want, find someone to love in your own time and on your own terms. No matter how badly they want to see you happy, throwing all these guys at you was never going to end well. I'm surprised you've put up with it this long. You're obviously a very caring daughter and niece. Most women I know would have told them to shove off already."

"I love my aunt. She's like my second mom and my idol all wrapped into one eccentric package. But her biggest regret in life is chasing her career for so long that she missed her chance to settle down and have children. I mean, she had her extended family around her, but she really pined for kids of her own. And since she sees a lot of herself in me, she's transferred her fears, I guess. I don't have it in me to be cruel and tell her to stop, you know?"

"Do you want what she wants for you?" I ask, my voice coming out softer than expected.

"Do I want a husband and kids? Well...yeah. Eventually. But I want it to happen naturally, you know? All this pressure..."

"Makes it hard to know how you really feel?"

She nods. "I just wish they'd be happy because

I'm happy. Regardless of whether there's a man involved."

"I totally understand," I say, as I glance at her again. My protective instincts flare brightly inside my chest, and somehow, I know that no matter how this day goes, I'll do whatever it takes to help her. I happen to know a little about the weight of someone else's expectations and the damage an interfering parent can do...

DELANEY

"Are you ready?" I whisper, blowing out a calming breath as I lift my hand to knock on my aunt's door. I don't know why my mother always calls this Aunty Joan's *house* when it's an actual *estate* with electric gates, an expansive circular driveway, and a butler to boot. While my aunt never got to have the family she wanted to fill the many rooms of her home, she certainly has an abundance of everything else this world has to offer.

"As I'll ever be." Nate takes a deep breath himself, his presence calming as he stands beside me with the pie balanced in one hand and our bags in the other. "You'll be fine," he assures me, flashing me one of his charming smiles as we hear footsteps from inside. "We've got this."

"Thanks," I say, just as the door opens and Aunty Joan's butler, John, ushers us in.

"Welcome, Miss. Gilchrist," he says, as we're relieved of the pie, our coats, and bags by the two maids standing by. "Sir." He gives Nate a polite nod.

"Thank you, John. Is everyone in the sitting room?" I ask, just as my mother comes rushing from that direction like she's being chased.

"You're here!" Mom says, her hands lifting as she makes her way forward and embraces me. "I thought I heard the door. How was the drive?"

"Long, but beautiful as always," I say, noting how high pitched my voice sounds as she looks from me to Nate.

"And this must be Liam." Her eyes shine bright as she clasps her hands in front of her. "It's just..." She pauses and shakes her head. I stop breathing. "It's so wonderful to finally meet you!" Nate doesn't even get a chance to respond before she's hugging him like the prodigal son returned then cupping his face in her hands like she can't trust her eyes. "He's so handsome!" She swings her gaze to me.

"And he has ears to hear you, a mouth to respond and everything," I say, trying not to laugh as Mom quickly releases Nate and titters—she genuinely *titters*.

"I'm so sorry, Liam. I'm just...wow." She smiles

as her eyes drink Nate in the same way I'm sure mine did when I met him. "You're not what we were expecting at all."

"What were you expecting?" Nate asks, smiling politely as he slides a hand around my waist and draws me to his side protectively.

Mom looks from him to me and back again, a look I can only describe as awe etched into her features. "You just look so handsome together." She sighs. "And I'm so glad you came. Everyone is dying to meet you. Come." She gestures for us to follow her as she turns for the sitting room. I don't miss the fact that she used the word 'handsome' over 'beautiful' to describe us, and I can't help but feel a little deflated by that. *Does she really think I'm that unattractive?*

"Where's that beautiful smile gone?" Nate whispers close to my ear as we follow behind. I'm keenly aware of the heat of his hand at the small of my back and the closeness of his body next to mine. It creates stirrings in me I didn't even know existed. But then all of it—my mother's shocked reaction to his good looks, and the fact she's right to *be* shocked—has only further highlighted how unrealistic this coupling really is. Nate is only here because I'm paying him. He's not here because he thinks I'm the sun and the moon. He's not here because I'm the first and last thing he thinks of each day. No. He's here for the money.

And I've never felt that truth as much as I do in this moment.

"Maybe…maybe we should go?" I whisper, stopping before we reach the other side of the foyer.

"Go?" Nate stops with me, his blue eyes searching mine as I have a mini panic attack.

"Is everything all right?" Mom asks when she realizes we aren't still walking with her.

"Everything's fine," Nate says quickly. "I think Delaney is just a little lightheaded after the drive. Can we get some water?"

"Oh, of course!" Mom says. "You haven't gotten car sick since you were little, sweetheart. Did you eat this morning?"

"I had a piece of toast, but that's all."

"John. Can we get some water here?" With both Mom and Nate so close, I feel too closed in. The lie I'm telling is looking right at me and it makes me feel ugly both inside and out.

"I need to—" I clap my hand over my mouth and run for the bathroom, closing myself in before I suck in big gulps of air and splash some water on my face. *I can't do this.* I thought I could, but I can't.

As I pat my face dry with a hand towel, I stare at myself in the mirror, trying to think of a way out of this. Then the door opens and closes and

Nate slips inside, crowding the small space with his size.

"Crisis of conscience?" he asks, moving in behind me.

I meet his eyes in the mirror and nod. "I'm not used to lying," I whisper. "And this...you and me...it's too unbelievable to be true."

He takes a slow inhale before he places his hands on my shoulders and turns me to face him. "Do you know what I thought when I met you?" He lowers his head slightly to look me right in the eyes, and I shake my head. "I thought, *wow*. That's it. One word. One syllable. Wow."

"Wow?" I frown, searching his eyes for more meaning. Wow could mean many things. From amazement to mockery and everything in between.

"Yeah," he says, tucking my hair behind my ear. "I thought, wow. How is *this* the woman Liz told me about?"

"You're just being kind because I'm paying you to be here," I say, offering a slight smile. "The truth of all this is that I'm quite pathetic and no one out there is ever going to believe *you* are dating *me*."

"Why? What makes this coupling so unbelievable to you?" He frowns like he genuinely doesn't understand.

"My god, Nate. Look at us," I say, whirling

around until I'm facing the mirror. "Something here doesn't fit."

He takes a deep breath as he studies our reflections carefully. "You're right," he says.

"See?" I hold up both my hands, relieved he's admitting it too. Maybe now we can figure out a way to leave before this lie gets any bigger.

"I do." He lifts a hand and tugs the tie from around his neck. "The blue of this tie looks hideous next to your dress." He pulls it free then shoves the length of it in his pants pocket. "Much better," he adds with a nod. "Don't you think?"

He flashes me a smile, and I can't help but laugh. "No. That wasn't what I meant at all."

"Then what? I think we look pretty great together now that god awful tie is out of the picture." He places his hands on my shoulders and leans a little closer, keeping his voice nice and low. "And I'll tell you something for free, Delaney. If I hadn't been meeting you to talk business the other day, I would've found a way to talk to you. And then I probably would've asked you out. So before you go listening to disparaging comments from passive-aggressive people, remember that. Because you are *exactly* the kind of girl I would go for."

He releases me and steps back, giving me a meaningful look via the mirror before he slips from the powder room, leaving me with my thoughts and the echoes of his words. Can I believe they're true? Or is he really just *that* good of an actor?

As I touch up my makeup, I come to realize that it doesn't matter. Because if the man can come in here and make *me* believe he finds me appealing, then it gives me the courage to trust that my family will believe him too. I'm not sure I'll have the gall to continue this farce for the sake of the cruise, but maybe, just maybe, I can get through Thanksgiving unscathed. I'll worry about the rest of this tomorrow. For now, I'm just going to go out there and allow myself to feel special with a gorgeous man on my arm—regardless of how he got there. I can pretend too.

NATE

When Delaney steps out of the bathroom, I entwine my fingers with hers and offer her an encouraging smile before we enter the room her relatives are gathered in. I'm offering moral support while also trying to reassure her that she's more attractive than she gives herself credit for. It pains me to see a beautiful woman so down on herself that the slightest insinuation from her mother rocks her confidence like that. It's unjust and undeserved, and at the very core of it, you can be damn sure the reason she feels that way is because she wasn't told she was pretty enough as she was growing up, so she's unaware of her worth. I feel like part of my job here should be to show her that. So I intend to be the best damn boyfriend she's ever had. So good in fact, that she might not want to let me go when this is through. *Can't say I hate that idea...*

"Liam, the dentist!" A dark-haired guy a few years older than Delaney—her brother, I'm guessing—announces our arrival like this is some kind of sideshow entertainment they've all been waiting for. I bristle slightly.

"That's me," I say as he approaches, and Delaney makes the introductions official.

"This is my oldest brother, Tony," she says, releasing my hand as Tony holds his out to shake mine.

"Tony." I greet him with a nod as I take it.

"Nice to meet you, man. This is my wife, Lucy, and our two kids, Mitchell and Anna." He points them all out and they offer up a little wave and a smile. "And this is Tommy—yes, we're twins—he and I were actually taking bets over whether you were real or not." Tony laughs then gives Delaney a wink, making my protective instincts burn even brighter. *I kinda want to hit him for that.*

"Why wouldn't I be real?" I ask, trying not to squeeze his hand too hard before I release it.

"Oh...no reason," he says with a smirk as he steps away. *I think I hate this guy.*

"For what it's worth, I was betting *for* you. Not against you," the next brother, Tommy, says as he slides in to take the place Tony just vacated. "I'm Tommy, and it's nice to finally meet you." He shakes my hand and smiles.

"You too," I say, deciding he's my favorite in the family so far.

"You sure this guy's good enough for you, sis?" he says to Delaney as he releases my hand then hugs her hello.

"I wouldn't have brought him if I didn't think so," she says with a somewhat relieved smile. "Where are Tarryn and the kids?"

"Home. Cory wasn't feeling too great so I'm going it alone this year."

"Oh no, give them my love," Delaney says as she rubs his shoulder with genuine affection.

"Of course, and they send theirs. Tarryn was bummed she wasn't going to get to meet your Mr. Right."

"Oh gosh, don't go putting that kind of pressure on him, Tommy," Delaney says with a roll of her eyes. "You'll send him packing."

"Wild horses couldn't drag me away," I interject, sliding a hand around her waist and pulling her in close. It feels right having her there. Like my side was made for the purpose of tucking her in and keeping her next to me.

"Good man," Tommy says. "Treat her right and I won't have to go all big brother on your ass." He says it with a smile on his face, but there's a seriousness in there too that I don't miss. To be honest, I'm happy to see it there. So far, my impression of Delaney's family hasn't been the greatest. Tommy seems to be the most invested in his little sister's happiness. If it ever came down to it, there's no way he'd beat me in a fight—I'm a good foot taller than him and broader than he will ever be—but I like that he insinuated the threat, shows he cares.

"I'll keep that in mind," I say as Delaney places her hand on my arm and urges me to move across the room to where her mother sits beside an older gentleman and who I'm guessing is this aunt Delaney doesn't want to disappoint, the family's matriarch, Joan.

"You've met my mom, Gladys," Delaney says as Gladys smiles up at me and nods regally. "And this is my dad, Roger..."

"Nice to meet you," I say, shaking his hand.

"...and *this* is my Aunty Joan," Delaney says of the white-haired lady with big glasses and even bigger beads hanging around her neck.

"Nice to meet you," I say, grinning as I hold my hand out to take hers. She uses it to stand, also pushing up on a bright pink walking stick.

"So, this is Liam," she says, looking me up and down and nodding approvingly before turning back to Gladys. "He looks like he has a really tight ass. Like you could bounce a quarter off it." She mimes the movement.

I open my mouth, smiling but unsure of how to respond to that one. It's not every day an elderly woman makes a comment about my ass. "Can't say I've tested my ass's abilities with quarters to give you a definitive answer on that one," I say eventually, earning myself a chuckle from around the room, mixed with a couple of surprised gasps.

Joan's shrewd eyes land on mine as a smile curves her painted pink lips. "I like this one, Delaney. Come, I want you both sitting either side of me." Joan slides her arm in the crook of mine and gestures for me to head into the dining room where there's a long table set up with gold-edged plates, crystal glasses, and gleaming cutlery.

The centerpiece is orange and white flowers with mini pumpkins and delicate vines curling out, making this the fanciest damn Thanksgiving I've ever taken part in. I realized when Delaney informed me there was a dress code that this wasn't your typical family gathering. But still, I wasn't expecting this level of opulence. I mean, there's a *butler and maids in uniform.*

"Now, why don't you tell me all about yourself, sweetcheeks," Joan says as we take our seats. The rest of the family seems a little put out that their usual seating arrangement is altered, but I just smile across at Delaney who's beaming with delight. This is obviously a big deal to her.

"What would you like to know?" I ask, giving the matriarch my full attention.

DELANEY

*D*inner goes off without a hitch. Aunty Joan says grace, thanking the Lord for bringing her family together and for sending us Liam—I find I can't keep my head bowed during that part, feeling uncomfortable bringing God in on my lie. But after that, we eat a meal of turkey, stuffing, potatoes, and deliciously prepared vegetables all smothered in a rich gravy while we drink wine, and we talk about the world, reflecting on the year and all we're grateful for.

Nate is a dream. He answers questions about himself, incorporating the backstory I provided him with while taking the time to shower me in praise, sharing the knowledge he gleaned from reading the 'about me' section in his character folder by telling them what an amazing business woman he thinks I am.

Any woman would be proud to have this man by her side, but it's tough for me to fully enjoy it when it just isn't true. The reason he's a *dream* is because I created him. I sat down and wrote out an entire folder filled with information about my ideal mate. Don't get me wrong, it's wonderful seeing the character of Liam being playing out in real life. But at the same time, it's bittersweet. My ideal man doesn't exist.

I grow quieter as the meal goes on. I love that I've finally been chosen to sit up at the head of the table with Aunty Joan. For a girl who was always chosen last for the softball team, the honor is quite grand. But it's hard to fully enjoy it when my acceptance into this coveted position is based on a lie. Nate is so entertaining, so attentive, and I enjoy just being in his presence and watching him interact with my family. But at the same time, I'm really struggling. And as the day wears on, I feel more and more certain that I won't be going through with this farce on the cruise as well. I know it'll break Aunty Joan's heart to find out that I lied, so I'll need to lie again to get out of this. But it has to end here. I don't have it in me to pretend for that long.

"Time for some fresh air," Aunty Joan says once the main course dishes are cleared away. "I could do with stretching my legs and letting this meal digest a little before we move on to dessert."

"Do you need help up?" Nate asks, jumping to her aid quicker than I can even register the movement.

"If I were thirty years younger, I'd steal you away as my toy boy," she says, gripping his strong arm as he helps her to her feet. "He's *so hot*." That last part is stage whispered for my benefit, and it makes me laugh.

"I agree," I say, pushing in her chair before I follow her and Nate out, really feeling how full my stomach is after that delicious turkey roast with all the trimmings. I blow out my breath and pat my stomach.

"Good meal, huh?" Tommy says as he moves alongside me.

"It was. And don't think I didn't notice how little you spoke throughout it. Feeling OK?"

He bounces a shoulder. "I'm fine. It's just strange being here without the wife and kids, you know?"

"I'm having the opposite problem. It's strange being here *with* someone." I gesture to where Nate is helping Aunty Joan relax in a white wooden lounger. Traditionally, we all come out to her manicured lawns to play a game of bocce between the main course and dessert. When we were little, all the kids and adults had a ball—literally—trying to get their bocce balls closest to the white pallino ball. We could be out here for hours playing against each other, but as we grew, we realized it was a great excuse for the adults to get liquored up while instilling some healthy competition between us kids. As our family has grown, the game and the sentiment is still the same. But now we have a new group of kids playing and more adults getting liquored up. Aunty Joan—who used to blitz the lot of us—no longer plays, preferring to take her enjoyment in observing with a cocktail in hand instead. She says the mint julip is to help with her digestion. But I've come to realize she's just a bit of a lush.

"I like him. I liked him when you first walked in because his body language was very protective of you, which really, is what you want when a guy is interested in your sister. But after listening to him at dinner, I reckon he's a pretty cool guy. Not the nerdy dentist type I was expecting at all."

"Dentists aren't nerdy," I say. "What gives you that impression?"

"Only every dentist I've ever met. The guy I see now has the personality of a wet mop. The one before him used to ask me a bunch of questions I could never answer because my mouth was wide open with a drill inside it, and the guy Mom took us to growing up just never spoke at all."

"I guess it's a hard job to get to know each other in," I say, realizing I hadn't given that part of my lie a lot of thought. "Maybe if you met them all outside of the office you'd have a different impression?"

"Maybe," he says, picking up a blue bocce ball and tapping his hand against the weight of it. "Point is, he seems pretty cool. Is he coming on the cruise no one's supposed to know about?"

"Maybe." This time I bounce a shoulder. "It's a bit hard this close to the holidays."

"You're telling me. Tarryn is pissed. If we go on this cruise it means she misses out on seeing her family for Christmas, and she's real close to her mom and sister. We've never skipped them before."

"I never thought of it like that," I say with a frown. "N—I mean...Liam, hasn't even mentioned Christmas with his family." I'm kicking myself for that almost slip up, but more than anything, I'm wondering what Nate's real situation is. He didn't even blink about the fact this cruise takes place over the holidays. Does he not have anyone to spend it with?

"Is he close to them?"

I shake my head. "He doesn't really talk about them."

"Well, you might want to get a read on that. Or you'll be in the doghouse like I am with Tarryn."

"Is that the real reason she isn't here today?"

"Yeah. She's spending Thanksgiving with her

family since they'll miss out on Christmas. Marriage is all about compromise, Del. You'll see."

I release a laugh and shake my head. "We're not ready for that yet."

"Try telling Aunty Joan that," he says, handing me the bocce ball. "If she gets her way, Liam will be proposing before the day is out, and believe me, that woman has some amazing convincing skills."

NATE

"So, what do I do with this game?" I ask, tossing the weighted red ball up and catching it again. Delany, holding a blue ball, takes a step away to show me. I have to fight the urge not to pull her closer again. The more time I spend with her, the less I like being apart.

"It's kind of like bowling. Except the goal is to get your ball as close to that little white one as possible."

"Closest wins?" I ask.

"That's right," she says, pulling her hand back and rolling the ball along the immaculate lawn. It taps against another ball and knocks it further away before it rests a few inches from the tiny white ball in the center.

"Oh, I see. We can play dirty by knocking each other's ball away?"

"Whatever gets you into the winning position."

"And what happens if you hit the white ball?"

"Well, if it's just a tap, nothing. If your ball rests against it, it's called a kiss." I waggle my eyebrows at that, and she laughs. "But if you hit it so hard it goes outside the boundary, then it's game over, and no one gets any points."

"OK," I say, moving into position so I can take my shot. "Let's see if I can get myself a kiss." That delicious heat brightens her cheeks as she smiles and drops her gaze. I'm so distracted looking at her that I release the ball and it just rolls across the lawn, completely missing the play zone.

"I'm sure you're really good at a great deal of things," Delaney says. "But bocce is not one of them."

"Hmm. You may be right," I say, watching as my ball finally comes to a rest at the edge of a flower bed. "Maybe you should show me your form again so I can pick up a couple of pointers?"

"OK," she says, picking up her ball and moving into position. "Keep your eyes on the space you want to occupy"—I know *exactly* what space I'd like to occupy—"then lean over and *gently* release." As she bowls, she's completely oblivious of the fact I'm standing directly behind her just to look at her ass when she leans forward.

We get four chances in this game and we're two in, so the next shot, I'll make sure I'm standing in front of her so I get a nice view of her cleavage. After that, it'll be a tossup what side of her I prefer a repeat performance of. I *really* enjoy looking at her.

"OK. Your turn again." She hands me a ball.

"Maybe you could…I don't know, lean over me like guys in movies do when they're showing girls how to play pool. I think that might help me with my aim," I tease, loving the way she giggles and tucks her hair behind her ear even though it's already off her face.

"Just roll the ball, slugger," she says, disappointingly keeping her distance.

I do as she says, and by the time the game is over, she's won by a mile, but I don't feel the loss at all since my dick is enjoying a gentle throb of attraction.

The longer we're here, the more I dislike the fact that I agreed to come here and act as this dude Liam. If I'd been even a tiny bit smart when I first met her, I would have told her I didn't want to pretend. That I wanted to date her for real. But now we're here, and I'm not sure how to change the dynamic without making Delaney look foolish—that's the last thing I want to do.

"You really do suck at this game," Delaney

says, grinning as we collect the balls and bring them back to their case.

"I might have been a teeny bit distracted," I admit, dropping the last ball into its allocated slot.

"With what? How big your muscles are?" She's teasing me, and I fucking love it.

"For your information," I say, grabbing her around the waist and pulling her flush against me. "I was distracted by how gorgeous you look in that dress you're wearing."

Her eyes turn from mirthful to serious as she whispers, "What are you doing?" with her hands pressed against my chest.

"Acting like your boyfriend," I murmur, bowing my head and brushing the tip of my nose to hers. "Is this too much?"

"Um." She swallows hard, her eyelids fluttering closed as her fingers flex then relax against my pecs. "Is this...what you would normally do?"

"Kiss my girl for whipping my ass in a ball game?" I hook a finger beneath her chin and lift until she opens her eyes and looks up at me. "Hell, yeah," I whisper, bringing my mouth to hers and gently sucking on her bottom lip. I want to wrap my arms around her and drive my tongue down her throat, devour her until she can't breathe anymore while I show her what I'd like to do with my dick, each time my tongue moves alongside hers. I want to possess her. I want to own her. And I never want to let her go. But... there are children around—not to mention her father is watching. So, I'm forced to keep things chaste. I'm forced to hold back, keeping our first kiss soft and all too brief.

"Well, you're certainly very good at doing that," she whispers as we part lips and she looks up at me, so flushed that my dick rears up, desperate for me to know exactly how far that blush goes.

"Just wait until I get a chance to kiss you properly. It'll curl your toes."

She giggles, and all I want to do is take her some place quiet and kiss some more, but Tony's kid, Mitchell, comes running across the yard yelling, "Desseeeeeeeeeert!" like he's a fucking airplane or something. He's cute and all, but his timing sucks.

"I think it's time for dessert," Delany says, smiling as she steps back from me and I'm forced to release her. In a way, I'm thankful. Dessert means we're one step away from this meal being over, one step away from being shown to our room, one step away from being alone together.

When we first agreed to this event, I'd planned to be a gentleman and sleep on the floor. But now...well, now I don't plan on being a gentleman at all....

DELANEY

"Now, you all know by now that I'm getting somewhat...*old*," Aunty Joan says after the dessert plates are taken away and the evening draws to a close. We're all stuffed full with pie and ice cream, so we've moved back into the sitting room for champagne to toast the day. She's standing by the mantle holding several envelopes in her hands. "I don't know how many more holidays I have left in me. But I decided recently that I wanted one last hurrah with everyone that I love close by. It makes me exceptionally happy to see my family happy, and I want to spoil you all rotten and see the joy it brings you with my own eyes." She smiles and hands the envelopes to her butler, and he passes them around the room. "So...what you'll find in your hands are tickets for a Holiday Cruise. Ten days of all-expenses-paid luxury on the Caribbean." Her eyes gleam and she claps her hands together in glee. It's like she's closer to being a schoolgirl than a ninety-five-year-old woman, and just seeing her so happy makes me smile. "We're going to have the most wonderful time."

"Thank you, Aunty Joan," I say, the first to get up and hug her. "This is truly generous."

"You're so welcome," she says, smiling brightly. "And you make sure you bring that dish of a man, Liam, too. There's a ticket in there for him." She winks. "I have a good feeling about him. He really cares for you."

"You think so?"

She nods. "I know so. He'll make you happy, petal. And when you're old like me, happiness is all that matters."

"Thank you," I whisper, stepping away so my brothers and parents can thank Aunty Joan themselves. It's an insanely generous gift, and I instantly feel bad for bemoaning it when I first found out about it.

For the first time in a very long time, I'm spending time with my family as a part of a couple instead of a thirty-six-year-old single woman they feel the need to fix. It's a very different dynamic, and while it's a dishonest one, it's given me the chance to see things in a different light. And I'm actually enjoying myself for a change. But that's largely to do with Nate. He's proving himself to be the best boyfriend money can buy.

"Looking forward to the cruise?" he asks, moving my hair to the side before lazily trailing his fingers along the exposed skin at my neck. It sends delicious chills throughout my body, and I have to take a sip of my drink to hide my reaction to him, although I worry that the satin of my dress is showing off the way my nipples have puckered under his touch. *Why didn't I choose a thicker bra?*

"I am." I smile as I swallow the remnants of the bubbles in my mouth. "How about you?"

"I'm more excited about seeing our room for the night." He smiles as his fingers trail down my spine.

"Oh? You're tired, are you?"

"Incredibly." Releasing a chuckle, he sets his champagne aside while I drain mine. The way he looks at me like I'm his next meal makes me nervous. I'm not sure how to react or how to feel, or even if this is real or just part of the show. Part of me wants to just let myself relax and enjoy the full breadth and depth of the boyfriend experience, and another part is screaming at me to slow down and keep my guard up. But as the night wears on, the champagne flows, and by the time we're up in our room, I'm not caring about how real or fake this thing is anymore. All I care about is that I want it. I want him. And I don't care if I'm paying for it.

"Here we are," I say, stepping inside the spacious guest bedroom in the east wing of Aunty Joan's home. I've frequented this room many times in the past, and she's always kept it decorated just for me, so the apricot wallpaper and the romantic black and white images of Paris at night are all here for my taste. It's part of what makes me love Aunty Joan so much. She genuinely cares about us all and will do anything to help make us feel loved in return.

"Beautiful," he says, although he's not talking about the room. His eyes are solely on me.

My heart hammers in my chest as I look up at him. "You're just saying that," I whisper, suddenly self-conscious now that we're alone and the lie doesn't have to exist anymore.

"I'm really not," he replies, sliding a hand around the back of my head and drawing me in close, pressing his mouth to mine. He keeps it quite still at first, our lips wrapped around each other's but caught in a freeze-frame as he inhales, and I react with a rigid body and a warring mind.

Can I really do this?

I feel frozen in that lip lock for an age, but in reality, it's probably a split second where I run the gamut of shock, fear, reasoning, and desire. It's when I reach that final point where I give in, my hands moving into his light brown hair, pulling it free from the elastic that kept it neat and bound all day. I take fistfuls of it and pull those luscious lips against mine as I open my mouth and let him in.

Tiny moans leave me as he kisses me deep and long, stealing my breath while his hands move over my body, grabbing and squeezing, pressing himself against me and showing me how ready he is for me. *Talk about customer service!*

He moves his mouth lower, his teeth grazing my chin before his mouth is on my chest, his hands kneading my breasts, lifting them high as he sucks against my skin. "Oh yes," I gasp, feeling sure he's marking me and loving the idea of that little souvenir from his magnificent mouth.

"I've been desperate to get you alone all day," he murmurs as he pushes my dress from my shoulders and presses wet kisses against bare skin. Inhaling deeply, I catch the scent of shampoo and a woodsy cologne, mixed with that manly smell that seems different from person to person. His scent has a certain panty-dropping quality to it that has me dripping wet and desperate to rip his clothes off and take him inside me.

"Lie on the bed."

He quirks a brow in response. And honestly, I'm as surprised at my emboldened command as he is. But there's something about knowing this isn't real that makes me feel like I can have anything I want, take and give *anything* that I want, and I've had just enough champagne that I feel brave enough to do it.

As he backs up to the foot of the bed, my hands move to his chest, and I shove him back with a strength I didn't know I had. He lands with a bounce on the mattress and grins at me before he presses up on his elbows then licks his lips while he eye-fucks my body. "Didn't take you for a bossy one," he says with a hungry smirk.

"I guess there's a lot you don't know about me," I say, climbing over him and pulling his shirt from his pants as I hold my mouth just close enough that our lips touch, but far enough away that each time he tries to kiss me, I pull back.

"Minx," he says as he lies back and watches me while I twist open each shirt button, pushing the expensive cotton open to reveal a tan, ripped torso that has me licking my lips.

"You look too good to be true," I whisper, nervous yet bold as my eyes drink him in. This situation has me feeling unlike myself as I give into my desires and run the tip of my tongue between every ridge of those perfectly sculpted muscles.

"And you're a fucking dream." He moans as I press my lips to his chest, sucking and licking between his curved pecs, running my tongue around his nipples then through the ridge that runs down the center of his abs. I release a moan of my own, feeling a pulse between my legs at the hard heat of his skin and the saltiness against my tongue.

"I need to taste you," I say, working my way down his body. I look up at him and unbutton his fly, sliding the zipper open. My heart hammers in my ears as I slide my hand inside and find an impressive cock, hard and ready for me—*me*, the girl who's always been so hard to love. And I know this has absolutely nothing to do with feelings that run that deep. But still, it's nice to *feel wanted* in this way. No matter what's behind it. "Is this OK?" I move my hand up and down his length.

"OK?" I find him watching me with a lusty gaze and parted lips. "This is fucking perfect, sweets. I'm *all* yours. You can do anything you like to me. Ask for anything you like *from* me."

I chew lightly at my bottom lip as I consider his words, deciding that kind of go-ahead is exactly what I need. *Here goes nothing.*

NATE

She pulls my pants low enough to make my cock spring free. It stands long, thick, and proud, my arousal beading on my tip as she licks her lips and looks at it with hungry eyes.

Never in my life have I wanted a woman the way I want Delaney. Everything about her turns me on. Her hair, her skin, her smile; the nervousness that tinges her touch, and the boldness that overrides her nerves. She's simply magnificent.

"Tell me if I'm doing it wrong," she says as she takes me in her hand and parts her lips.

"As long as you don't bite, you can't do a bad job, gorgeous."

My head lolls back as she draws me into her mouth, swallowing me down until her lips kiss my base.

"Holy fuck," I hiss, my hands going into her

hair as my back lifts off the mattress. *Who is this woman? And where has she been all my life?*

The muscles in my neck strain. And I do everything I can to calm my breathing so I don't embarrass myself by coming too early. She looks up at me with those big blues as she works my shaft, humming and taking me deeper, sucking back harder. I can barely hold back, my fingers flexing, pulling her hair tight as I lose my ever-loving mind. *I don't want to come in her mouth.*

With a growl, I release her hair then drag her off me, flipping her onto her back and pinning her in place. I hold myself above her, my hands wrapped around her wrists.

"My turn," I grunt, crashing my lips to hers as I kiss her deep and long, my hands releasing her wrists and moving down her body to the hem of her dress.

As my fingers move along the milky skin of her thighs, her breathing speeds up and her fingers fist the sheets. My dick is still out, and I trail it along her inner thigh, loving the way she opens up to welcome me.

"Do it," she says.

"Not yet." Gripping her hips, I flip her onto her belly, pulling the zipper of her dress down to the top of her ass like I'm unwrapping a gift Christmas morning. I've never been the type to hurriedly tear the paper away. No. I've always opened each gift with careful precision and Delaney is no exception. I push the fabric open, brushing my fingers over her warm back before I unclasp her bra then press my mouth against the curve of her neck, trailing kisses over her exposed skin until I'm at the dimples that reside where her ass meets her back. "On your knees."

She does as I ask, faint noises of need escaping her throat as I pull her dress and bra from her body, tugging her panties down at the same time, revealing her delectable nakedness and the delicate curve of her ass.

I release a groan as my hands move over her smooth cheeks, admiring how round and fleshy they are before I move my fingers lower, teasing her seam as I lean forward and press my teeth into her cheek. At the same time, my fingers enter her, two digits encased in her warmth as I run my tongue along the marks my teeth left. It was more of a nip than a bite, but I couldn't help myself. She's just too delicious not to mark.

"You're so tight and wet, Delaney. I can't wait to be inside you."

"Oh, God," she moans, her hips swaying against me, letting me know she's ready for more than I'm giving her. "Please, Liam. *Please*."

Immediately, I stop. "Did you just call me Liam?" I ask, hoping to fuck I heard wrong.

"I...w-was that wrong?" she stammers.

Withdrawing from her body, I tuck myself away and button up my pants. "That's not my name."

She moves to the edge of the bed, pulling the blanket around her body. "I'm sorry. I thought...I thought this was part of it."

I shake my head, running a hand through my hair. "I don't have sex for money, Delaney. That's not who I am."

"I'm sorry, Nate. I...I didn't realize this was...I didn't think—"

"I'm going to take a walk." I hold my hand up to stop her, grabbing my shirt and tugging it back on before I head for the door, shoes in hand. I need to calm the fuck down.

"Wait." She stands and crosses the room, the blanket around her. "What if someone sees you?"

"Then they'll think we're a couple having an argument. Your secret is safe, Delaney. Don't worry your pretty head about the hired help."

"That's not what...Nate!"

Her voice follows me as a whispered hiss as I stalk down the hall, but it disappears entirely by the time I get to the stairs. With my blood pumping through my ears, I quickly descend the marble steps, heading out through the side doors into the lawn area we played bocce on earlier.

"*Fuck,*" I mutter as I drop my weight in one of the lawn chairs. I'm still barefoot, and something about putting my fucking shoes back on pisses me off even more. I toss them, one by one, throwing the second harder than the first because it just feels good to put that power behind it. I just came from almost having sex with Delaney and I'm frustrated and...I'm hurt. I honestly thought I'd made it clear to her that I, Nate Charmers, was interested in her when we were in the bathroom earlier in the day, then again when I kissed her on the lawn, touched her in the sitting room. Sure, I've been playing the part of her boyfriend all day, but besides a few basic facts about who I am and how we met, the rest of it was just me. *I'm the man who wants her.*

But does she want me?

"Did you just throw your shoes?" a voice asks on my left, causing me to jump since I thought I was alone—seems I'm getting a lot of things wrong today. I turn my head and find the orange glow of a lit cigarette, my eyes making out the outline of one of Delaney's brothers.

"Tommy?"

The orange light glows brighter as he inhales. "The one and only. Couldn't sleep."

"A lot of that going around," I say, as he gets up and moves to sit in the chair beside me.

"Well, you're still dressed for dinner, so I'm guessing lover's tiff. Especially since your shirt is hanging out and the buttons aren't straight."

I look down and realize my collar is askew and I've missed a couple of buttons entirely. "Just a misunderstanding," I say, looking at my palms as I replay the moment over and over in my head. *Please, Liam. Please.*

"I know all about those." He chuckles as he shakes out another cigarette and lights it off the butt of the first one. Then he offers the pack to me.

"No thanks," I say. "Don't smoke."

"No one does, anymore," he says, blowing his stream of smoke in the opposite direction to me. "It's why I do it in the middle of the night so no one ever sees me. I trust you'll keep this to yourself."

"Your secret is safe with me."

"As is yours," he says, and my gaze snaps to his as he relaxes back and inhales deeply.

"What secret?" I ask, my brow knitting.

"The one where you're not a dentist, but an actor called Nathanial Charmers she hired to play the dutiful boyfriend."

"She told you that?"

"No. I just thought you looked really familiar. Took me most of dinner to place you. See, I kept picturing you in an orange jumpsuit, and I didn't know why. Then it hit me—my wife loves legal dramas. You were in an episode of Law & Order. So I looked you up. Impressive resume."

"I don't know if I should be flattered you recognized me or threatening you to keep your mouth shut for your sister's sake," I say. Despite my current situation with Delaney, I'm still protective of her.

"That's Tony you'd need to threaten. Not me. I've got plenty of secrets of my own to worry about, I don't need to be outing Del for hers. To be honest, I'm glad she brought you along. Lord knows they've put her through enough with their incessant matchmaking."

"Why do you think they do it?" I ask, noticing the scent of whisky mixed with his tobacco.

"Fucked if I know. They say it's about our happiness, but I think it's got a lot to do with control and money. Everyone wants a piece of this after the old Aunty is gone." He nods toward the mansion behind us. "They all think that doing whatever she asks will get them a bigger slice of pie. But I don't think that's the case at all." He frowns and looks at his cigarette, twisting it between his fingers. "Want to know an even bigger secret to trump the fact you're an actor?"

"Lay it on me."

"She's leaving this place to charity. Specifically, the Children's Defense Fund. Since she never had kids of her own, she wants her legacy helping kids who are less fortunate than the rest of us. She donates buttloads as it is, but in the end, she's leaving this to them. The rest of us..." He laughs before he sucks on his cigarette. "We get nothing but a few knick-knacks and pieces of art." The chuckle continues as he blows out the smoke from his lungs. "Don't get me wrong here, I love Aunty Joan, she's the most pure of heart human besides Delaney that I know, but when she passes, I'm going to enjoy watching the faces of my parents and brother when they find out that all that ass-kissing, all the bullshit pretense was for fucking nothing."

"How did you find this out?"

"She asked me to be the executor of her Will, so I had to sign it and swear I'd do everything she asked."

"Why do you think she chose you to do that and not your mom?"

He grins. "Because Aunty Joan isn't a stupid woman. I mean, look around you, do you think she did all this without knowing *exactly* how to read people?"

"How *did* she do all this?"

"Candy," he says.

"Candy?"

"Yup." He pops the P. "Candy."

"Wow. I was wondering obviously, but I never imagined..."

"Right? But sugar is big business, and Aunty Joan is as sweet as pie, but she's got the mind of a steel trap, and she's as shrewd as can be. She turned something very small into something huge, and for all her smiles and generosity, she's incredibly aware of the intent of those around her."

"So...if she knows, why does she keep allowing it to happen?"

"Because it's family. And without all of us, she'd be horribly lonely. Which is where that regret of hers stems from. She thinks that if she had kids of her own, my parents and Tony wouldn't look at her with dollar signs in their eyes."

"And you don't? Look at her with dollar signs, I mean?" It's a confronting question, but since we're throwing stones...

He smiles. "I did. But then I got married, had kids of my own, and my wife pointed out how fucked up it is to look at someone as a paycheck when they die. Delaney is the only one of us who *never* did that. She just loved Aunty Joan for Aunty Joan. She's never cared about the money or the doors Aunty Joan could open for her. She's always gone out there and done everything for herself, never asking for help from any one of us. She and Tony have their issues—he's never understood why she won't just fall in line, and he truly thinks Aunty Joan is leaving the lion's share to her—but I've always thought she was so brave. It's a big thing to start from scratch on your own in a brand-new city. But she did it and her business is thriving as a result of *her* brains and skill. I think that's why Aunty Joan cares so much about Delaney. She sees a lot of herself in her and wants to make sure she has everything she didn't. It's why she pushes the husband thing so fiercely. She wants Del to have kids while she's still young enough to have them."

"Has anyone even asked her if she wants that?"

Leaning forward, he puts the butt of his cigarette out in the cool the grass, the tiny flame dying out with a hiss. "Interestingly, no. You must think this family is pretty messed up."

"I've seen worse. There are some doozies in Hollywood, and my own wasn't a treat either. But I do have to wonder why you're telling me this. I mean, you're aware this relationship between me and Delaney is fake, and I'm not a priest, so..." I shrug.

He takes a long inhale then stretches his arms behind his head, looking up at the night sky. "Because we're all pretending here, Nathanial Charmers. And the only honesty I see is in the way you look at Del. I guess this is just my big brother way of letting you know what you're getting yourself into, and asking you, no—telling you—to do right by her. I don't want to see her getting hurt."

"What if she's the one with the power to hurt me?" I ask, looking back up at the house and thinking about the moments before she called me Liam, how it felt to be close to her, how she reacted to my touch, how she made me feel. I've never had that before. *But it wasn't real.*

"Then god help you, buddy," Tommy says. "Because I certainly can't."

DELANEY

It's my bladder that wakes me. Light streams in through the window and the uncomfortable nagging sensation forces me from my deep, restful sleep. Getting to this point wasn't easy. After Nate left last night, I had a bit of a cry, then I had a shower and cried a little more, and then I got into my warm pajamas and curled up in bed, crying a little there too. I felt, in a word, *awful*! This big, beautiful, and caring man was showing me the most divine time of my life and what do I do? I treat him like a hooker—the very thing I assured Liz I wasn't going to do.

In my defense, I'd been calling him Liam all day. So the name could have very easily slipped out in the throes of ecstasy. But in truth, it wasn't a simple faux pas on my part, I called him Liam because I thought he was still *pretending* to want me. After the way he reacted though, I think that maybe I was very wrong. Which can only mean one thing—*Nate* wants *me*. Something I never imagined would be possible. And I fear that acting like he was providing a service to me last night might have damaged that want.

Especially since I find him sleeping on the sofa—shirtless with the blanket riding low on his waist, his hair loose and spread out on the pillow in a way that makes me want to reach out and run my fingers through it—instead of on the bed next to me. *Crap. You really blew this one, Delaney.* And not in the hot, deep throat kinda way. No. If I were a betting woman, I'd bet that was never going to happen again.

I don't know why finding him on the couch bothers me so much. I mean, it's not like he's ever slept in the same bed as me before. I'm not used to having him beside me all night and waking up next to him of a morning. So there's no *real* reason for my disappointment besides the fact it feels a lot like a change of heart. Like maybe, last night was my only chance, and I blew it the moment I uttered the wrong name.

God, I could kick myself for ruining this!

Nate is the first man to set my blood pumping like that in, well, *ever*. And stupid, incapable-of-reading-the-signs me, managed to screw that up before we even got to the good part. *Nice one,*

Delaney. Maybe you should stick to making skincare products and call this relationship thing a day? It'd probably be safer for all of us.

Beating myself up internally, I drag my feet into the bathroom and do my business, splashing water on my face before I comb my hair and start getting ready for the day. Nate and I have a long drive back to the city, and I don't want to hang around any longer than I need to, especially when things are just going to be uncomfortable from now on. I'm not even sure *how* I'm supposed to look him in the eye now, or what I can say to make it better. Quite simply, I fucked up.

With my hair in a ponytail, my jeans and a knit sweater on, I pull my walking shoes on then take one last look at the slumbering Nate before I head downstairs to get some breakfast.

"Where's, lover boy?" Tony asks from where he sits at the table slathering a bagel with cream cheese.

"Where are Lucy and the kids?" I retort, grabbing a blueberry muffin as I take a seat across from him. I love my family, even the hard to be around ones like Tony, but today, I'm not in the mood.

"Sleeping."

"Then I guess that answers your question too."

He grins in a way that reminds me of a snake

as he takes a bite and chews rather rambunctiously, keeping his eyes on me like somehow there's a mystery to be solved here. "You in a fight?"

"Why would we be in a fight?" I ask, focusing on the crumbs that have fallen on my plate so I don't need to meet his eyes and have him see the lies in mine. I'm just stressed enough that I might blurt it all out, confessing to the worst possible person in the family.

Tony and Tommy are like two sides of the same coin. One side is truth, and the other side is dare. Tommy, of course, is truth. If I ever have a problem or need an understanding ear, he's the one I would go to. Tony, on the other hand, is dare. He thrives on stirring the pot. One time when I was a senior in high school, I snuck out to a concert with my friends, and he caught me sneaking back inside. He swore black and blue that he wouldn't say a word, and in a way he didn't, but he did make sure my parents found my ticket stub so I was found out anyway. I don't think I've ever really forgiven him for that. I got grounded for a month and missed out on my senior trip to the snowfields, all because I trusted the wrong person. No wonder I have issues with men.

"Good morning, sweet girl," Dad says as he enters the dining room. He's wearing a pair of tailored pants and a button-up shirt like he always does. There's no room for casualness with my dad. He believes that every day matters as much as the one before, so you should look the part. I don't think the man owns a single pair of sweats, and any T-shirt in his drawer is of the undershirt variety, never to be worn in front of company. "Good morning, son." He takes a seat at his usual spot and collects fruit and a croissant from the serving dishes in front of us. "I trust you both slept well."

"Like a log," Tony says, patting his stomach as he pushes back from the table. "Do you know where Aunty Joan and Mom are? I want to say goodbye and thank Aunty for her generosity before we hit the road."

"Outside. Joan wanted to walk before she sat down to breakfast. They'll be back soon."

"Might try and catch them then."

"I thought the kids were still asleep," I say, narrowing my eyes slightly.

"Sleeping, packing. Same thing." Tony gives me a wink as he tugs his pants up over his middle-aged paunch and heads out. Mom says it's the sign of a happy man, so I wonder what that says about Tommy who's still as slim as he ever was. Is he *not* happy just because he didn't put on weight? And what about me? I've always been big. Am I to be perpetually jolly?

"And what about your fellow?" Dad asks, turning to me and cutting into my fat versus happy internal debate. "Where is he off to this morning?"

"Oh, he's still—"

"I'm right here," Nate says, coming up behind me like a panther in the night. He smells like a fresh shower and soap as he presses a kiss to the side of my head. "Good morning, darling." He smiles at me and takes his seat. But the smile doesn't touch his eyes the way it did yesterday. And the way he moves is just...stiff. *Oh...* I dare say I just learned the difference between Nate acting like he cares and *actually* caring. Today he's acting. Before...he wasn't. *I miss him already.*

As Nate and Dad make small talk about the weather and football, I choke down the rest of my muffin, barely tasting it as I try to figure out how one apologizes for calling an actor the wrong name during sex. I mean, it's not like Hallmark has a range for that, do they? So, I'm going to have to get creative here. Luckily, we have a whole ten-day cruise to try and figure it out.

NATE

"I...I want to apologize for last night," Delaney starts when I pull up outside her apartment building. The car is still running, and the air between us is tense. We've barely spoken a word the entire journey back. It's not that I don't want to talk to her. It's just that I'm trying to wrap my head around what I want and how I'm supposed to make that happen. But no matter what way I look at this, one of us loses. Either I spend my life pretending to be a dentist called Liam, or Delaney comes clean with her family. And I just don't see a world where either of those scenarios works—not to mention the fact that she's shown no real, *tangible* feelings toward me, Nate, during these past thirty hours. So, I'd really rather not speak at all unless I'm in the process of playing the part I was hired to play.

"You don't need to," I say, my hands gripping the steering wheel as I keep my eyes straight forward. "I understand why it happened. You don't need to explain." That's my biggest problem. If she truly thought what happened between us last night was part of the show, there's no way she shares the same kind of feelings toward me that I do toward her. And I have no right to be upset over it. I came into this knowing it was a business transaction. Hell, I have a folder full of information telling me it was one. I shouldn't be shocked that a brilliant, successful woman would prefer to pretend with me instead of build something real. At the end of the day, I'm no catch. I'm a man living in his friend's guestroom because I failed at my dream and I have absolutely nothing to show for it. What could she ever want with me? I'm a failure who can act. She's an entrepreneur who stands on her own two feet. *One of these things does not look like the other...*

"I feel like I do need to explain," she says, biting her bottom lip nervously. "You seem angry, and it wasn't my intention to upset you. Just want to say that I'm sorry and I'll understand if you just want to call it quits from here. I'll tell them we broke up and I'll pay Aunty Joan back for the ticket. It's fine." *And that's me dumped.* At least now I know where I stand.

"Our agreement was Thanksgiving and a ten-day cruise," I say, forcing myself to look at her and keep my voice even. "I'm a professional, Delaney. You've paid for a devoted boyfriend, and a devoted boyfriend is what you'll get."

"I see. Then I suppose I'll see you on the sixteenth for the cruise?"

"What happened to meeting up to work on our relationship story between now and then?"

"I'll send you any notes I make," she says, pulling open the door. "Like you said, you're a professional. You don't need me to micromanage you."

"For what it's worth, Delaney," I say, causing her to pause before she slams the door shut again. "I enjoyed being your boyfriend yesterday."

Indecision crosses her features as she holds my gaze for a beat. "I enjoyed it too," she returns, her chin lifting as something resembling pride takes hold. "And I apologize again for misunderstanding your intentions. It won't happen again." With a curt nod, she closes the door and makes a beeline for her building's entrance. I sit in the car until I can't see her anymore, wondering at what point in the last thirty hours I managed to fall in love with her. *This is going to get messy.*

DELANEY

"Why don't you just tell me what happened," Liz says as she bites the end off a candy cane and stares up at me with those doe eyes of hers. "You've been in a bad mood ever since you got back from Thanksgiving and frankly, 'tis the season to be jolly, and you're bumming me out." She gives me a pointed look from where she sits at my dining table with her feet stretched across two chairs.

"I told you. It's embarrassing," I mutter, holding my bright floral bathing suit up and stretching it across my body, wondering if it's still going to fit—I've gained a few pounds in recent weeks from stress eating. I've been in denial for days, but now that I'm packing for the cruise, I'm rethinking asking for extra whipped cream on my mint-flavored mocha each morning, as well as the half-pint of ice cream I ate most days. Ugh. Why does food have to make you feel good when you feel crappy then hang around like a bad memory on your hips? It's unfair.

"As embarrassing as that time your bra broke, and your boob fell out of your dress on New Years?"

I scrunch my bathers up and toss them into my suitcase where it sits open on the table. "Worse."

"Worse? Wow. It must be bad." She places her feet on the floor then leans forward, resting her elbows on the table. "Was it a *sex* thing?"

My cheeks burn as I roll up a silk kaftan and throw it in my bag as well. "We've been through this before, Liz. I really don't want to talk about it."

"I wish you would. Nate is being tight-lipped too—believe me, I nagged Burt until he promised to grill Nate for me, and he's keeping the details close to his chest. Did he…" She shifts her eyes side to side then lowers her voice before she continues, "fail to, you know, rise to the occasion?" She tilts the candy cane up to mime getting an erection.

"No! He had no issue in that department," I blurt, feeling horrified by the idea. Something like that would have truly destroyed my self-confidence. As it is, my confidence is somewhat emboldened, however my conscience feels like shit.

"So it *was* a sex thing!" She gasps, jumping on my slip up like a kid at a piñata party. "I *knew it*. Tell me more? Was he too small? Too big? Crooked? A premature jizzer?" She fires questions off in quick succession.

"What? *No*. None of those things."

"Then what? You have to talk about it some time. It's obviously eating you up, Del. I'm your best friend. If anyone is going to understand you, it's me."

"I..." I start, picking up a handful of random T-shirts and dropping them into my suitcase along with most of the contents of my underwear drawer. I'm not even sure what I have anymore, just that throwing things in makes me feel productive.

"You what?"

Swallowing hard, I lift my eyes to hers and open my mouth. "I called him Liam."

She frowns. "Isn't that who you hired him to play?"

"Yes. But it's *when* I said it that's the problem. We were...fooling around and I...I thought he was doing it because I'm paying him to want me but he wasn't, and oh god, Liz, he's the first man I've ever been completely attracted to, and I blew it. He barely even spoke to me after. I treated him like a prostitute." It all comes out in a rush once I start, and now I'm just trying not to cry about it.

"Oh, hun." Liz gets up and moves around the table, wrapping me in a tight hug. "Why didn't you just tell me this? I'm sure you didn't mean to say the wrong name. It would have been an easy slip up after calling him Liam all day."

"But, it wasn't an accident. I did it on purpose. I just…I didn't think a man like him would want me. That's why it's so awful. Then he just froze, told me he doesn't have sex for money and left."

She pulls back and looks me in the eyes. "What's so wrong with a girl like you?"

"Liz," I say, exasperation in my voice because I hate having to point this out. People act like being overweight is the 'thing that shall not be named'. Like, just acknowledge the fact I'm a bigger than normal woman and move on. "My own mother keeps setting me up with men who need glasses. If that doesn't tell you I'm unsightly, nothing will."

"But you're not," she argues. "Jesus, Del, you have no idea how gorgeous you are. OK, so you're above average size, but big is the new beautiful, and your hair is naturally the color people pay big bucks to emulate, and your skin—oh my god, don't even get me started on how flawless your skin is. You're like one of the porcelain dolls my grandmother used to collect. And then you have beautiful eyes and a smile that makes even my heart weep—and I actually hate cutesy things—so from where I'm standing, you're a total catch. And I know, *I know*, you weren't trying to hurt Nate's feelings or treat him like *he sells his body to the night.*" She's doing the Count Von Count voice again, and it's actually making me smile despite myself.

"You're an idiot." I wipe at my eyes and shake my head at her affectionately.

"An idiot who got you to laugh, right?" she says, smiling as she taps me under the chin.

"Yeah. The best kind."

"And since we know you're the best kind of idiot too, maybe we can stop beating ourselves up over Nate. You're about to go on a ten day cruise with the man. So it's not over. You just need to talk to him, be open and honest, explain why you felt the way you did, and I'm sure he'll understand."

"What if he doesn't?" I ask, frowning with worry.

"Then he's a giant butthead and we don't like him anymore."

Leaning in, I wrap my arms around her in a big bear hug. "I wish you were coming on this cruise too."

"Someone's gotta stay behind and keep the

business going. But you go and have some fun. Let go of all that bullshit baggage your parents gave you and figure out that you are a beautiful goddess with a heart of gold. Any man worth your time will see that. Thank me by making me a godmother to your gorgeous blue-eyed babies."

"We're getting a little ahead of ourselves here, but sure. You'll be godmother to all my babies. Including the company."

She straightens her back and holds her hand up in salute. "Your business is safe with me, Captain!"

I laugh at my quirky best friend, knowing that I'm truly blessed to have someone like her in my life. Then I get back to packing my suitcase and going over the work schedule for while I'm gone. It's not easy leaving the business I've built from the ground up in the hands of someone else, but I know she's up for the challenge. Now, all I have to do is get to the port on time and figure out a way to make Nate understand my insecurities and forgive me. One is easy, the other requires bearing my soul and trusting he won't crush it. Now *that* is terrifying.

NATE

*A*fter I thank the Uber driver, I straighten up and sling my duffel bag over my shoulder, scanning the crowd at the dock for Delaney's flaming-red hair. It's been almost three weeks since Thanksgiving, and the only contact I've had with her is a single email containing the cruise itinerary and a handful of anecdotes about our 'relationship'. I replied with a simple thank you then sat there and thought about her all day.

And all night.

And every moment since.

I feel like she's everything I want but can't have. The fact that the couple we have presented to the world so far is different from the people we are is the single greatest hurdle we face. Sure, I could play the part of Liam in front of her family for the rest of my life if I needed to. But how is that going to bode well for the longevity of a relationship between the real me and Delaney? There'd be this constant undercurrent of fear that we slip up and her family would find out, and it would end up tearing us apart. And if there's one thing I've learned about Delaney Gilchrist, it's that her family means everything to her. She literally created a fake boyfriend so she wouldn't have to offend them by telling them to back up off her with their insistence she get married and have kids in the next five minutes. I swear, it's all her mother hinted at whenever we spoke.

Honestly, I don't know why Delaney does it. Besides her aunt and Tommy, I don't see a lot of true caring between those people. It's just a bunch of poor fitting masks with fake smiles and selfish intentions, sponging off an old woman's generosity. They should be ashamed of themselves.

It doesn't take long before my eyes find their target. Delaney's hair shines bright in the sun, attracting me like a beacon. The time away from her has given me a chance to reflect on what happened between us at Thanksgiving, and to make some decisions about how I need to separate my desire from my work going forward.

Did I overreact when she called me the wrong name when we were messing around? Maybe. Probably.

Did I make it clear that I wanted her as a man and not as her character? Maybe. Probably not.

And that's probably where my mistake lies. I assumed she understood how I felt about her, while she just thought I was playing a part. The end result, I felt cheap. I felt used. I felt misunderstood. And honestly, I've had enough of that in my life.

The best course of action from now until the end of this cruise is to keep things completely professional between us. I'm not willing to live a lie all my life, so if there are any feelings toward me on her side, she'll need to come clean with her family first. Otherwise, we just can't be.

I want her so much it boils my blood, and as much as we all say that when it comes to love, we're willing to do anything for it, in the great words of Meatloaf, 'I won't do that.' I won't pretend to be a dentist called Liam for the sake of her greedy family. For me, it's all or nothing. Call me cruel, call me stubborn, or even call me stupid, but as far as I'm concerned, in matters of the heart, if you don't have honesty, you don't have anything at all.

"Hey." Delaney does a nervous tuck of her hair as she smiles up at me when I approach. She's wearing a peacock blue and fuchsia patterned kaftan dress that's cinched in at the waist and looks like summer on a cold but sunny day. She's also got a thick coat on that seems at odds with the tropical fabric, but that's also in a bright fuchsia and matches her ensemble perfectly. I'm also starting to think fuchsia is her favorite color since I've seen it on her a couple of times now.

"Hey, yourself." I offer her a smile before I take a hold of her hand and lace our fingers together. Her eyes go to our joined hands then back up to mine. I give her fingers a gentle squeeze to let her know we're OK. "Still want to go through with this?"

"Want and need are two very different things," she says, her tone sounding somewhat relieved.

"So no plans to come clean and tell them who I really am?"

"Oh, lord. No. I couldn't. They'd be so upset with me. And Aunty Joan...I can't admit I lied to her." She lowers her voice to a whisper on that last part, and it's really all I needed to know.

"OK. Liam it is. Let's just keep things professional this time so we know where we stand. Does that work for you?"

Her eyes drop to our joined hands again. I can't tell if she's disappointed or wishing I'd let her go. "If that's what you want." Her eyes return to mine. "Should we lay down some ground rules? Maybe that's where we went wrong before. It's something I probably should have thought about when I emailed you."

"Ground rules...I think...yeah, let's agree to some of those. In public we're together. In private, we're not. Hand holding is obviously OK." I lift our hands in example.

"OK." She licks her pretty lips as she scans the surrounding crowd, no doubt checking to make sure none of her family members are in hearing range. "And what about dancing? We'll need to touch and embrace so we look appropriately *into* each other. If we're suddenly not all touchy-feely like we were at Thanksgiving they'll for sure know something is up."

"Do you ever get tired of worrying about what they'll think?" I ask suddenly, unable to hold back.

Her mouth drops open but quickly closes as she frowns and searches my eyes. "What do you mean?"

"Exactly that. Don't you just want to tell them to get fucked so you can live your own life on your terms?"

She gasps. "They're my *family*."

"And if they were *my* family," I say, leaning in close to her ear. "I'd tell them to get fucked."

"Well, they're *not* your family," she snaps, pulling her hand from mine. "And if that's the way you feel then maybe you—"

"Hello, darlings!" Aunty Joan's voice cuts into Delaney's tirade before she can finish, and I take the opportunity to snatch her hand back in mine and pull her nice and close. She might be unwilling to change the terms of our relationship where her family is concerned, but Liam likes to shower his girl with affection—something we established at Thanksgiving, as Delaney so helpfully pointed out. And if this game of pretend is all she's willing to give me, then so be it. I'll dote on her like she's never known.

"Aunty Joan," I say, holding out my free arm and embracing the old woman while Delaney gets her game face on. "How has your gorgeous self been these past few weeks?"

"Trawling for toy boys on Tinder," she says with a completely straight face. "But all they want to do is send me pictures of their penises—dick-pics I believe they're called—and I didn't even ask for them. What I'm interested in is the amount of muscles they have because my old lady hooch has had quite enough plundering for one life. I want to look and admire. I don't want to actually *do* anything. Maybe what I should do is go trawling for men at the local gym? Find some pumped up fella who's obviously been on that roid stuff that shrinks your bit. Can't imagine they'd want to show me photos of their junk before we even talk, am I right?" She elbows me in the side and cackles at her own story. "Yes. I think that's exactly what I'll do."

"Aunty Joan," Delaney says with a smile as she

wiggles her hand from my grip and embraces her aunt. "What on earth made you think Tinder would be a good place to hang out?"

"Oh, I overheard the maids talking about it, so I got John to download it and set up an account for me. It was just for a bit of fun. I'm not getting any younger, you know. Got to have all the fun I can before it's too late."

"Is there something you aren't telling us?" Delaney asks when she holds her aunt at arm's length and scrutinizes her. "This cruise. Now Tinder. You're actually starting to worry me here."

"Oh, child. I've just realized that time is getting away from me and I don't feel like I've had enough fun. I'm old and I'm eccentric, so now is the best time to *act* like it. Live your best life is what the young kids say, right?" She looks to me for confirmation, and I nod.

"As long as that's all it is."

"I promise you," Joan says, placing a comforting hand on Delaney's arm. "Now, your father and mother are just off checking in all of our luggage so we can move through to the boarding area. You two should probably go and do that yourselves and meet me back here."

"I'll go," I volunteer, leaning down to pick up both mine and Delaney's bags from where they sit on the ground. "You two stick together. It's easy to find Delaney in a crowd."

"Because I'm so big?" she snaps, her eyes flashing and exciting me at the same time.

"No, gorgeous. Because of your red hair," I say, giving it a gentle pull before I lean in and kiss her on the cheek, giving her a final wink before I step away. "I'll be back soon."

"Take your time, my love," she shoots back, giving me a smile that doesn't touch her eyes. *Something tells me this cruise is going to be a lot more fun than I thought it would be.*

DELANEY

We're welcomed onto the ship with a string quartet playing Christmas music and servers offering glasses of champagne, whiskey or eggnog. The festive season is all around us, and Nate laughs at me because I keep craning my neck looking at all the decorations and displays. He has to keep steering me through the crowd, so I don't bump into anybody. But I can't help it, Christmas is my favorite time of year.

I did wonder if being on a tropical cruise would make it feel less like the holiday, but after seeing the splendor around us, I have to think this could very well turn out to be the best Christmas I've ever had. All of my family is in one spot, and the man I'm crushing hard-core on is by my side.

Now all I need is a miracle. And Christmas is the perfect time for them, right? If somehow Saint Nick himself wants to smile down on me and give me a clue as to how I win Nate's heart, then I will be forever grateful. Because despite the 'keep it business' line on the dock, my attraction levels are at least ten times higher than they were at Thanksgiving. I don't know how it happened, but I swear that man got better looking. I *need* him in my life. I just need to work out how to go about it. Our circumstances aren't normal. If I could wish for one thing this Christmas, I'd like to get my man and escape my family unjudged—which is why I need the miracle.

By the time we get into our room, it's almost time for dinner. My face hurts from smiling so much and my stomach aches from wanting so much. Having Nate glued to my side being so attentive has been intoxicating. But I've noticed there's this wall up around him now that wasn't there before. I gives me a deep-seated longing for the ability to turn back time and redo Thanksgiving with different intentions, but the line has been cast now, and I guess I have to work with the fish I caught. *Ugh.* That's a horrible analogy, but I think we all get the gist—I've got regret over the last time we were together. I've got longing from the time in between. And now I don't know where to start since Nate, despite his acting abilities and attentiveness, still seems pissed at me. The words, *'let's just keep things professional this time'* keep ringing in my ears and casting doubt over my hopefulness.

What if I don't want to keep things professional?

What if I want things to get dirty like they did last time? I could say the right name this time and everything...

Feeling the familiar tightening in my belly that occurs every time I think about him touching me like that, I close my eyes for a second and sit on the edge of the bed to take my shoes off. We have to get ready for dinner soon, and I'm not really ready to face my family again just yet. I love them all, but an afternoon spent touring the ship and talking non-stop has me exhausted. I'd like to curl up on this bed and just sleep until I don't feel tired anymore. *Wait. Do I hear...snoring?*

Opening my eyes, I find Nate stretched out on the couch, napping like he doesn't have a care in the world. His long, muscular frame too big for the space he's using, but somehow, he seems completely comfortable and at ease. *How is it that I miss him even though he was never mine?*

Letting out a sigh, I put my feet on the plush carpet and wriggle my toes. Aunty Joan got us a suite with a balcony, a full-sized bathroom, and walk-in closet. With the lush furnishings and the perfect view, I'm feeling rather spoiled, indeed.

Forcing myself back into my sore feet, I make my way into the walk-in and find our suitcases in there, sitting on the plush sea-blue bench seat that adorns the center. As I unzip mine, my eyes stray to Nate's. I don't know why, but I have this itch to see what he has in there. Is it all board shorts and Hawaiian shirts? Or did he pack for every possibility?

The thought rattles around in my mind as I fill the racks and drawers with my possessions and slide the empty suitcase into the provided slot beneath the shoe rack on my side. So by the time I've finished, I've convinced myself that unpacking for him as well is just a kind thing to do.

"It's not *snooping*," I say to myself as I pull open the zip on his duffel. "It's helping."

One by one, I remove the clothing from his bag, hanging up his dress shirts and pants—points for thinking about dinner attire—and placing his casual wear and boxers in the drawers. I'd be lying if I said I didn't hold his soft white T-shirt to my nose and inhale his scent, letting it flow through my body along with the memory of what he tasted and felt like when I took him into my mouth. *My clit aches just thinking about it.*

Pulling out his shoes, I pause when I find the

folder I gave him during our first meeting on the bottom. When I take it out and flip through it, he's printed out and added the suggestions and anecdotes I emailed through, along with some handwritten notes of his own: *takes two sugars in her coffee. Doesn't seem to like green beans or pumpkin pie even though she's the one who brought it. Talks in her sleep. Favorite color?* My heart swells as I read his words, freezing when I find a comment further down the page, *doesn't think she's lovable.*

Instantly tears prickle my eyes at the confronting words, and I put the folder back inside, not wanting to risk reading anymore. There's a saying about opinions—everyone has one, and what's theirs doesn't belong to you. I don't need or want to know what he secretly thinks of me. If it turns out he agrees with that statement, well, I don't think I could even try to pretend with him then.

Just as I tuck the folder away in the duffel, a hard plastic tube rolls sideways and taps me on the hand. For a brief moment, I wonder why Nate would bring a flashlight on a cruise. *Is he afraid of the dark?* But then I pick it up and notice it has a cap. My breath catches. I know what it is before I remove the lid, but still, I take the damn thing off and find myself face to er....vulva of a fleshlight.

Oddly, I contemplate putting my fingers inside it to see how similar to the real thing it actually is. I've never seen one up close before, but before I can make a decision on that, the clearing of a throat causes me to yelp and spin around.

"Nate!" My eyes go wide as I meet his, the embarrassing evidence still in my hand and open. "I-I...I thought you were sleeping?" I do my best to act normal as I cap it and shove it behind my back.

"What do you have there, Delaney?" he asks with a smirk. My cheeks flame.

"Absolutely nothing," I squeak, trying to laugh it off.

"Nothing?" He lifts his brows and glances over my shoulder, which is where a big full-length mirror adorns the wall. *Oh shit. Forgot about that.*

"I, uh, was just...unpacking!" Not one to admit defeat, I tilt back and flick the damn thing behind me, hoping to get it in the open duffel.

"Unpacking my fleshlight?" he asks, his eyes following the tube as it rolls right off the bench and lands on the floor, the tilt of the ship allowing it to tumble across the carpet right toward him like a little traitor of lady parts everywhere.

"I thought it was a torch," I quip, my voice high and tight as my face burns so bright I think I smell BBQ in here.

"A torch?" He releases a chuckle as he bends

down to pick it up. "I guess it *does* make me see flashing lights."

"I'm sure it's glorious," I say, clearing my throat as I turn around and zip up his bag. "But I fail to see why you'd need it on a ten day cruise."

"A man has needs, Delaney," he says as he opens a drawer and throws it in like this isn't the slightest bit embarrassing for him at all.

"Couldn't you just use your hand if you were that desperate?"

"I could." He meets my eyes as he steps toward me, closing the distance between us as my nipples decide to stand up and take notice. "But when I fuck, I like it tight and wet and silky smooth. My hand can be tight and it can be wet, but these things are rough as fuck. As you'd well know."

"You should really get some moisturizer for them," I whisper, my voice deep and lusty as the memory of those rough hands touching me plays out in my mind. "I have some. My...my company makes it." I gulp and lift my eyes to his as his gaze drops to my lips.

"You'd moisturize my hands for me?" he murmurs, leaning in so close I feel the heat of his skin and the warmth of his breath. I shudder.

"If it's what you wanted." I breathe as everything in me tingles with anticipation. You know, I really should have hired a less delicious man to play the role of Liam. Once, I went to Vegas for a bachelorette weekend and saw that show, Thunder from Down Under. The guy looks like he belongs in something like that, dancing shirtless while women scream at him adoringly.

"What I want?" He lowers his head just enough that our lips brush, sending a spark roaring through me, right before he says, "I don't think you can give me what I want," and pulls back.

I blink twice, staring at him in confusion as I try to catch my breath. "What is it you want?" I ask.

But Nate doesn't even get to open his mouth before there's a knock on our cabin door.

"Open up!" Tony calls out, his voice muted. "My kids are making me nuts, and my wife won't let me raid the mini bar."

"I'm coming," I call back, tearing my eyes from Nate's as I move to go and open the door.

He catches me by the arm. "Ignore him."

I glance up and swallow hard. "He's my brother," I whisper before I pull my arm free and take a deep breath to compose myself before I let Tony inside. Nate disappears into the bathroom.

NATE

"He thinks you don't like him," Delaney says as Tony leaves our cabin and she leans against the door. He just spent the last hour in here complaining about his wife and kids while letting us know that his cabin is much bigger than ours and comes equipped with a slide for the kids to get down from the second level. Personally, I don't give a shit how big anyone's cabin is. The man is insufferable.

"That's because I don't," I say, pulling my hair off the back of my neck and winding an elastic about it as I walk into the closet. We have to be at dinner in about twenty minutes, and neither of us is ready.

"You could pretend," she says, following me. "Isn't that part of this?"

"I was pretending," I return, reaching for my

dress shirt and sliding it over the white T-shirt I put on after taking a quick shower to calm down after my run-in with Delaney. I was so close to kissing her—properly—which is something I promised myself I wouldn't do unless she's willing to drop this farce. "It just so happens that Liam dislikes him too."

"How convenient," she says, and I'm surprised to hear a smile in her voice. I turn around to find her stepping into a new deep-blue dress, her silky black underwear on display along with her abundant curves. My dick goes hard, and I have to look away before that fleshlight becomes the only thing that'll save me.

Grabbing my pants from the hanger, I quickly drop my sweats and pull them on, adjust myself to look less out of control as I do the fly up. "Any boyfriend who gives a shit about his girl would show disdain for the way Tony treats you. That jab he made at Thanksgiving about betting that your boyfriend was imaginary was enough to rub me the wrong way."

"He was only joking. It's just his big brother way."

"Tommy behaves like a big brother," I say, turning to find her struggling with her zip. "Tony behaves like a schoolyard bully." She turns abruptly when she realizes my voice is directly behind her. "Let me help."

Sucking in a breath, she turns her face forward and pulls her luscious hair over her right shoulder, her breathing obviously faster as I pull the zipper upward. "Is there anyone else in my family you hate?" she asks.

"Hate is a strong word. Dislike is more on point. I dislike Tony. And I also dislike your mother." I lean in closer while I secure the hook and eye at the top of the zip.

"My mother?" She whirls around to face me. "What's wrong with her?"

"I surprised her," I say, meeting her deep blue eyes. The fabric of the dress makes them look sapphire.

"Surprised? When?"

"When we arrived. She said I wasn't what she expected then you got all uncomfortable and decided no one was ever going to believe I chose a woman like you. That's when we stood in the bathroom mirror." I touch her shoulders and spin her around so we're facing the long mirror in the closet. "And I told you you're *exactly* the kind of girl I'd go for." Our eyes meet in the mirror and hold. It's like I can see her remembering the moment, realization dawning as she understands that every time we were alone, I wasn't playing a part. I wanted her all along.

"Nate," she whispers, her hand reaching up to touch mine.

I pull away and clear my throat. "I'll meet you at the bar when you're ready."

"Ah, sure," she says, frowning slightly before I slip my feet into a pair of loafers then head on out, realizing that this sexual tension between us isn't just going to go away or be ignored. No. It's a living, breathing thing that seems to grow whenever we're near. Being strictly professional is going to prove more difficult than I thought. I want her too much. In fact, I need her. Forever. And I won't accept anything less.

DELANEY

*D*inner goes as expected. Nate is on his best behavior playing Liam, and if one didn't know any better, they'd say Liam is a dream. Which is exactly what my sisters-in-law say when we're waiting at the bar for the after-dinner festivities to start. My parents are seated to the side with Aunty Joan, looking mortified while Aunty chats up a waiter in her gregarious way. I'm standing with Lucy and Tarryn while Nate is at the bar getting me a gin and tonic and himself a beer. While he's occupied and we're on our own, Lucy and Tarryn take the opportunity to gush about how amazing they think he is.

"How in the world did you land a man like that?" Lucy asks, her mouth agape as she drags her eyes over Nate's back. I don't miss the fact that she lingers a little too long while looking at his ass.

"What do you mean, 'how did she land him'?" Tarryn asks, frowning as she sips on her wine spritzer. Tommy has gone back to their cabin with the kids since neither of them is comfortable leaving them in the care of the ship's staff at night. Lucy and Tony don't have the same problem, but their kids are a little bit older and not as attached as Tarryn and Tommy's are, so Tony is lined up at the bar with Nate. *I'll bet Nate hates—I mean, dislikes—that.*

"I was just saying that you don't often find men who look like him wandering around willy-nilly," Lucy explains. "He could be a model, maybe even a fitness trainer. But a dentist...I've never seen a dentist that hot before."

"Neither have I," I say, smiling but keeping my answer short.

"So, he's not just a stripper who dresses as a dentist?" Lucy giggles.

"You're being insensitive, Luce," Tarryn says. "And you're dismissing how intelligent the man obviously is by only focusing on his looks."

"I'm just...*really* jealous." Lucy giggles before turning her attention to Tony who is returning with her wine.

"What are you girls gasbagging about?" Tony asks.

"Delaney was just telling us how she and Liam got together," Lucy says, winking at me as she takes a big gulp of red.

"I was?" I blink a few times as I try to recall all the details. I mean, I know the story—I did write it after all—but it feels very different writing it down and saying it out loud while trying to sound convincing.

"Yes! I want to hear this," Tarryn says, tapping my arm gently. "You didn't tell us at Thanksgiving."

"Oh...that's because there isn't a huge amount to tell," I say. "We met at the supermarket, got talking and the rest is history." I flash them a smile and bounce my shoulders.

"It was a little more than that," Nate says as he slides into the conversation, handing me my drink before returning to his possessive hold about my waist. I have to say I do enjoy this part of our *business* relationship. I know he made it very clear that we wouldn't cross that line from business to pleasure again. But I am still holding out some hope that he'll give me another chance. Those couple of incidences in our cabin felt so filled with tension that I wondered if he was about to kiss me.

"It was?" I ask, shooting a look of warning his way. *Don't elaborate on something we can't prove!* He just grins and nods as he takes a mouthful of his drink.

"Of course, it was her hair I noticed first," he starts. "I was buying bananas, and as I looked up, I saw this flame-haired beauty pushing an empty shopping cart through the entry. I spent the next twenty minutes following along behind her and grabbing random items from the shelves to put in my basket so I didn't look like the creeper I was actually being. It was like there was this sweetness in the air around her. Something that I couldn't quite put my finger on. Vanilla, maybe. Oranges? Possibly just her. No matter what it was, I was drawn in. That much was clear. I had this uncanny need to know her, be with her. And eventually, after collecting at least twelve products I definitely didn't need, I worked up the courage to speak to her in the frozen food aisle. She was buying green peas, if I remember correctly. I walked up to her and asked if she was single. When she said she was, I asked her if she'd like to go out sometime. She responded by pressing those peas to her forehead like she was suffering from a head wound before she asked if I was serious. I'd never seen anything so adorable in all my life. She was so humble and unaware of her own beauty." He turns to me and meets my eyes, his voice soft and intimate. "I think that's what made me fall in love with her."

Clean up in aisle three! A woman is down! I'm seriously swooning here. Thank god Nate has his arm around me still because I can't trust my knees not to buckle without support.

"Aww. That is *so* lovely," Tarryn says, smiling wide. "You definitely tell that story better, Liam. Del, you held out on us *so much* there."

"Oh, you know me," I start, finding that my voice is shaky. I clear my throat before continuing. "I get embarrassed. I felt silly over the pea thing."

"Oh," Lucy says as she reaches out and gives my arm a squeeze. "That was the *best* part. You guys are so adorable. And when I see you like this, the way you look at each other, the way you *hold* each other...it makes me sick to my stomach." She bursts out laughing. "But in the best possible way. Oh my god, why don't we have a gorgeous meet-cute like that?" She directs that last part to Tony as she taps the back of her hand against his chest.

"Because we met at a party in college when you were dancing on the table, and I was looking up your skirt," he says.

"We were both drunk off our asses," Lucy continues. "And it took us a year of drunken hookups before we decided we were perfect for each other." They turn to each other and start smooching, and it's kind of gross. But I like that for all their brashness, they're still very in love with each other.

"College is an entirely different ballgame," Tarryn says, trying to tear her eyes away from Tony and Lucy. It's kinda like trying not to look at a train wreck. "Tommy and I were in the same study group. He was shy. I wasn't. I asked him out, and we've been together ever since." She flashes us a smile and shrugs in the same way I did. And I wonder if she's feeling lonely right now with Tommy back in the cabin with the kids.

"I actually really like the story of how you two got together. Tarryn didn't know that Tommy had a twin," I say to Nate. "She thought that he was ignoring her when she said hi to him outside of class. But it was Tony she was talking to, and he had no idea who she was."

"I was ridiculously embarrassed when I found out," Tarryn says. "It almost stopped me from wanting to date him."

"I can imagine," Nate says, smiling. "I remember having trouble with twins when I was growing up too."

I'm eager to hear his story, but it gets cut short when we're called into the theatre for the evening show. We wait for my parents and Aunty Joan as they make their way toward us. Aunty Joan has set up an itinerary that involves a new show every night. She wants us to have dinner together and to spend the evening together. The rest of the time is our own, bar a few activities here and there—like Christmas Day, for example.

Since she's the one footing the bill, I don't mind attending her choice of shows. The ship offers a wide selection, so we aren't doing the same thing every night. And she selected shows with a lot of variety. Tonight we are listening to live music, and tomorrow we're seeing a magician. She's also selected dance shows and themed party nights. So there's something for everyone. I think she's done a great job, despite a few of the protests I've heard.

"After you," Nate rumbles near my ear as we're ushered inside. Something about the intimate way he speaks has my body on fire. *This is going to be a very long ten days.*

∽

WHEN THE SHOW IS OVER, and the family has all said our goodbyes, we do a quick check in on Tommy who isn't actually disappointed he missed the music. "Had it been a Led Zeppelin tribute band, I would have been all over it. But piano?" He mimes a yawn. "Count me out, guys. Thanks for taking one for the team, boo," he says to Tarryn before kissing her on the cheek.

"I liked it," she says with a smile. "And I

enjoyed the company, so I was happy to. Thanks for walking me back, guys. We'll see you around tomorrow?"

"Absolutely," I say, leaning in to give her a kiss on the cheek before hugging my brother. "You two sleep well."

"Wish I could say the same for you," Tommy says, giving Nate a wink before he closes the door. And that's the moment Nate drops my hand.

The short walk from Tommy and Tarryn's cabin to ours is, in a word, quiet. If I were to pick another one, it'd be uncomfortable. We don't say anything. Not until we get into the cabin and Nate starts pulling the couch apart to lift out the sofa bed inside.

"We could share the main bed," I say, noticing how small that thing is compared to the rest of him. "Those things are always horribly uncomfortable, and this bed is huge. We're adults. It doesn't have to mean anything."

"I think we've already proven that we don't do so great acting like adults," he says, his voice flat as he disappears into the walk-in and returns with blankets and a pillow. "I'll be fine here."

"Well then, how about you take the bed and I'll sleep there. Or we can alternate each night. Keep it fair."

He pauses his bed-making and turns to meet my eyes. "I'm fine here."

"OK," I whisper before I grab my toiletries bag and PJs then head into the bathroom, taking a quick shower to wash the evening as well as my hopes away. The man is so mercurial. I can't figure out if we're up or down, in or out. I'd thought there was still something there from the way he acted earlier in the evening, but now, after spending the last few hours glued to my side, it seems as though he can't wait to get away from me. It's confusing to say the least.

By the time I'm finished in the bathroom, running through my skincare routine and braiding my long hair, Nate is already lying in the fold-out bed, his back toward me as I pad across the room and get into the massive circular bed on my own. I feel lost in it as I pull back the blankets and climb inside. And I feel more alone than ever knowing the one person I've ever truly wanted isn't that far away from me. *Pity he doesn't seem to want me anymore.*

"Is it because I put on weight?" I ask suddenly, wincing once the words have left my mouth. *How needy can you be?*

"What?" He rolls onto his back and lifts his head to look at me in the dimly lit room.

"I...I asked if the reason you were so quick to move away from me tonight was because I've put on weight since Thanksgiving."

"No," he answers simply.

"Was it because you hate me now?" I stare up at the ceiling as I listen for his voice.

"No. It's just the opposite."

I push up on my elbows and frown in his direction. "I don't understand."

"It doesn't matter, Delaney. Just get some sleep."

"It does matter. What do you mean?"

He releases a sigh and shifts to a sitting position. "You hired me to play a role. To your family, I'm Liam. I'm always going to be Liam. That's why how I feel about you doesn't matter. I'm not Liam. I'm Nate. And what I want from you can't happen because of that."

"What do you want from me?" I ask, my voice coming out in a whisper because I'm afraid of the answer and what it'll mean for me.

"You don't want to know."

"I do, Nate. I *really* do."

"Fine. But remember you opened this can of worms. It'll be up to you to decide what you do with them all."

"OK," I say, secretly smiling since he just used a lame fishing analogy too.

I sit forward, and he meets my eyes. It feels like it takes an age before he finally speaks, but when he does, I'm blown away.

"I want to own you, Delaney. Claim you, possess you, make you mine and never let you go.

I think you're the most beautiful woman I've ever seen in my life, and I have struggled going through a moment since meeting you where I haven't had you on my mind. So being close to you, knowing I can't have you the way I want you, is difficult."

"You *can* have me," I whisper, my voice wavering and afraid of the implications of the words I'm speaking.

"That's where you're wrong, Delaney. You and I aren't going to happen. Not unless you're willing to tell your family the truth."

"You want me to tell them you're an actor I hired?" I ask, dread filling the pit of my stomach.

"Is it such a terrible request?" he fires back. "I don't want you for a moment. I want you in *every* moment. And I'm not willing to lie and pretend I'm Liam for the rest of my life just to get it. I'm sorry if that's hard for you, or if I'm adding pressure to a difficult situation. But it's how I feel, and I won't compromise on that. It's all or nothing for me in this. I'm sorry." He lies back on his bed and rolls to his side, effectively ending the conversation while leaving me completely speechless.

With my mind reeling from his admission and his words, I lie back, polarized as I stare up at the ceiling. *Nate wants me.* And not only does he want me, but he wants *to own me.* Holy fuck. It's like a dream come true, but it's one that could very well cost me my family. I've always felt that their acceptance of me balanced on a knife's edge, and the moment I stepped outside my designated box, that acceptance would disappear along with their respect, and I'd be cast out on my own, excluded and unwanted. The idea is positively frightening to me. And even if they did accept the truth, admitting to them that I hired Nate to pretend to be my boyfriend would be humiliating. But...I'd have Nate. Maybe I could weather that storm knowing I have him to return to each day. Except then, Aunty Joan would be hurt and devastated by my lie, and I don't want to do that to her. But, *Nate*.... God, I have everything and nothing all at the same time. I curse the decision to hire a stand-in while at the same time celebrating it because it's the reason Nate and I met. Looks like I've got a hell of a lot of soul searching to do before I can make a decision on what comes next. Actually, who the hell am I even kidding? I've been feeling awful without Nate in my life since Thanksgiving, and no one in my family was even around to check in on me or notice. Why am I basing my decisions on them, when I'm the one who has to live with the consequences?

Back when I was talking to Liz, I wanted to know what I needed to do to win Nate back, and this is it. So, I'll tell my family tomorrow at dinner. They can react however they want. I want Nate more than I care about their opinions.

For the first time in my adult life, I actually feel like I'm coming into my own. And if I'm really lucky, pretty soon I'll be coming with Nate too—*pun intended.*

NATE

I sleep better than expected. But I didn't sleep for long. Instead, I spent an inordinate amount of time looking out the big balcony window, watching the deep blue sea kiss the cloudless sky as it turns from night to day. The entire time, I'm wishing I had Delaney in my arms.

Admitting my feelings to Delaney in the dimly lit room last night wasn't part of the plan, but it also wasn't something I could hold inside much longer. Being close to her is hard, and previous to coming here, I thought I could handle it. Turns out I'm not as in control as I thought I was. Turns out, I'm not in control of a lot of things. Least of all my feelings toward my cabin mate.

Having her ask me if the reason I didn't want to touch her anymore was because she'd put on weight, tore me up inside. I almost quit all pretense in that moment and caved to my desire to go to her and hold her close. The kind of conditioning that causes that kind of self-doubt is deep-seated and unnecessary, and I never want her to feel unworthy or unpretty or undesirable ever again.

Now I feel like it's my mission to convince her to risk it all and give us a shot. I understand that her family is important. But I also understand that a family's love is meant to be unconditional.

Regardless of how she gets there, her happiness should be all that matters. And I believe I'm the one who can make her happy. *She belongs with me.*

"Nate. Are you awake?" Her voice is a delicate whisper that pulls me from my thoughts.

"I am now," I say, rolling onto my back and finding her standing right next to my bed with a pad of paper in hand. "Holy fuck." I clutch my hand to my chest, my heart thundering against my ribs. "What the hell are you doing right there?"

"I couldn't sleep," she says, offering me one of her innocently beautiful smiles. "I stayed up most the night thinking about the things you said." *Now she has my attention.*

"And?" I sit up so my forearms are resting across my knees.

"And I made some... script changes if you will," she says, holding out the notepad in her hand.

"Script changes?"

She nods as I take the papers from her and read over her impeccably neat writing.

Scene: breakfast. Delaney (playing herself) and Nate (playing himself) go to the dining hall farthest from their cabin to ensure their privacy.

Nate (thinking he's still playing Liam): OK. You've got me here. What is it you needed to say?

Delaney: I spent a lot of time last night doing some soul searching, and I feel like I owe you an apology for even asking you to do this in the first place. I was attracted to you the first time we met, and looking back now, I realize that the feeling was mutual. You made it very clear that you wanted me with the direct yet sweet things you said to me, and I was too caught up in my own head to see or accept it. I treated you like a sex worker when I called you by the wrong name at Thanksgiving. And I'd do anything to take that back. If I was anywhere near as brave in love as I am in business, I would have told you last night that I want you too. Not as Liam but as Nate, the only man who's ever truly seen me. The only man I've ever truly wanted. And if you'll still have me, I'm willing to tell everyone at dinner tonight that I made you up. I don't care what they think. I've been the dutiful daughter, sister, and niece for thirty-six years. So now it's time to do some-

thing selfish for me, and to hopefully start something wonderful with you. What do you say? Do you want to be mine forever instead of just the holidays?

I turn the page, eager for more words. But what I find is just blank lined paper.

"This is the part where you ad-lib," she says, looking at me with nervous yet eager eyes.

"Can I have a pen?" I ask, watching her carefully as she rushes to the small table and plucks it from the surface, and returns to me, handing it over. "I have a few changes of my own."

"Of course," she whispers, twisting her fingers together as she waits for me to edit her script. It only takes a moment before I hand it back to her and watch the smile take over her face. "You changed the scene to right here." She flips the page just like I did. "But you didn't write any lines."

"That's because I'm supposed to ad-lib," I say, reaching out and grabbing her arm before tugging her onto the bed and into my arms. The notepad goes fluttering to the floor, and she lands against me like she's in a trust fall. Then I maneuver us so she's on her back and I'm holding myself on top of her, looking down at her beautiful face, her hair sprawled out across the pillow like a fiery veil. *I want to remember her like this always.*

"I like your ad-libbing," she whispers.

I lean down and brush my lips against hers.

"And I like you." She smiles, and I kiss her. Slow at first, but then deep and long as she opens her mouth and allows me to slide my tongue inside.

My entire body lights up like it knows this is what it's been missing all these years. "For the record, gorgeous, you don't owe me an apology for anything. I'm here by choice. I thought I could keep it professional. But I can't. So it's me who owes you an apology. Except I'm not sorry. I just want you too damn much."

"Then take me," she whispers as my mouth trails along her jaw, sucking lightly on her ear. "I'm yours."

"Mine, huh?" I move my mouth to hers and run my tongue along the seam. "Can I get that in writing?"

She smiles against my lips. "Give me the pen."

"Later. Right now, I want you naked with your legs spread wide." I push her dressing gown from her shoulders, my fingers bunching her silk slip about her waist as I search for her skin while she wriggles beneath me, helping me remove her clothes.

When all that's left is her cotton panties, she places her hands on my bare chest and whispers my name, "Nate." It's crazy how happy hearing her say my name while naked makes me.

"I'm in love with you," I blurt, my eyes moving between hers as she smiles.

"I'm in love with you too."

"Yeah?"

"Yeah."

"Say my name."

"Nate."

"Again."

She giggles. "I love you, Nate."

"Perfect," I whisper before lowering my mouth to hers and kissing her until her nails are pressing into my back and my dick is throbbing. "Now comes the fun part. Roll over."

"On my knees?"

"Uh-huh. Time to finish what we started at Thanksgiving."

She grins, and I release a rumble of appreciation as I sit back on my knees and watch her move, my eyes taking in her mountainous breasts as they sway with her movement.

"Fuck, you're beautiful," I rasp as I run my hands over her thighs and the curve of her ass before sliding up her back then down to the waist of her panties. "So soft and smooth to touch." I press a kiss against the small of her back before I hook my thumbs into the sides of her panties and...tear.

"*No!*" she gasps as they flutter to the floor. "They were my most comfortable sleeping pair!"

I lean over her, my erection pressing into her back as I slide my fingers into the back of her hair then angle her head so she's looking at me. "Then I have a new ground rule—no panties in the bedroom. That way, you won't need them. Or, better yet, quit wearing panties altogether." Then I crash my lips against hers, her taste flooding my senses. She whimpers, twisting herself around until she's wrapped around me, her hands going to the waist of my boxers and urging me to take them off. "Please, Nate. I need you inside me."

"Soon. I want to play first." Sliding my hands under her ass, I lift her off the pull-out and carry her to the big bed, giving us a hell of a lot more room—not to mention comfort—as I place her down gently. Then I continue to fuck her mouth with my tongue and twist her nipples with my fingers.

"Nate, please. I'm aching for you."

"Not yet," I growl, smiling at her impatience as I drag my lips against her jaw and down her neck, sucking on her breasts as my hands roam all over her skin and she writhes beneath me.

"Please. I need to come."

Still wearing my boxers, I press my erection between her parted thighs. "So impatient," I chuckle before the heat of her apex causes me to moan. "So hot." I shift down her body and position myself so my face is right between her legs and take a moment to admire her glistening seam. "This is what I wanted to do to you at Thanksgiving. I swear I've dreamed of touching you every night since." My dick jumps as I run my hand down her mound, teasing either side of her pink lips.

"I've dreamed of you too."

"Did you pleasure yourself thinking about me?"

"Yes," she whispers like she's taking a risk in telling me. It makes me want her even more.

"Me too," I say as I slip one thick finger into her depths and we both moan at the same time. "I imagined just what it would be like touching you right here as I touched myself."

"How does it compare?"

"Nothing compares to the real thing," I say as I look up and meet her eyes. "And my imagination never let me do this." I don't give her the chance to process what that meant before I'm clamping my mouth over her clit, my tongue swirling around the tight bundle of nerves as my fingers move inside, pumping in and out as she moans and whispers while she pulls on my hair and presses her thighs around my head, hips moving, fucking my face. I love every moment of it.

"Holy shit! Oh god! Nate!" Her orgasm hits so fast that I'm almost not ready for it. But I curl my arms around her thighs, holding her against my mouth as I double down, forcing those moans to turn into screams as her back arches off the bed and she explodes against my face again. "Holy fuuuuuuuck!"

She pulls my hair like the reins of a horse as I slow the movement of my tongue and fingers, bringing her back down to earth. The moment she releases her grip on my hair, I lift my head and take a much-needed breath as I wipe my hand over my mouth and grin down at my gorgeous Delaney. "*Now* I'm going to fuck you."

DELANEY

"You can let me know if I'm as good as your fleshlight," I tease as Nate removes his boxers and climbs over me, kissing and sucking until his face is aligned with mine and the tip of his cock is pressed against my center.

"There's no competition, gorgeous," he murmurs, pressing nibbling kisses to my lips as his tip glides against my slick entrance. He moans. "I'm not even inside you yet, and I know you win. Because I love you, you're perfect and real, and as far as that contraption is concerned, I plan to throw it off the balcony for the sharks to fuck. You never know, it might make them happier."

"Maybe." I giggle, placing my hands against

his muscular chest and loving the sensation. "I think it's really kind of you to share your toys."

He releases a laugh, his blue eyes shining with mirth. "As long as I never have to share you."

"Never," I whisper, feeling happier than I have in a very long time. "I'm all yours."

"All mine. Then let's say goodbye to Liam Tribiani," he says, pushing inside me and stretching my walls. It takes a moment for me to adjust to his thick girth, and I moan at the sensation, my eyes rolling back in my head from pleasure.

"And hello to Nate Charmers. Oh, God, that feels good," I hiss once he's fully seated. "I feel so...full."

"Hmmm. You're so tight, gorgeous. Better than I imagined." He places a hand at the base of my neck then trails his fingertips down the center of my torso, all the way to my stomach, then lower until he's tracing circles around my clit. "Think you can come again?"

I nod, my body feeling alive and on fire in the most delicious of ways.

"That's my girl." He hums pleasurably as he pushes his cock a little deeper before dragging back, excruciatingly slow, his eyes never leaving mine while his fingers continue to tease. "Feel good?"

"Wonderful," I force out as he slams back in with one fluid motion, grinding his pelvis against mine and making everything inside me stand up and sing Jingle Bells, like it was Santa himself who sent this early Christmas miracle to me, a reward for my many years of waiting for the right one. "Oh, Nate."

"Delaney. Tell me you're mine. I want to hear you say it while I'm fucking you."

"I'm yours, Nate. I was yours in that café, and I'll be yours until I die. I love you. I love you. I—" Every fiber in my body shudders as he moves. Back and forth, long, languid strokes as he circles my clit, around and around, applying the perfect amount of pressure until he has me screaming again. "Holy shit!"

He groans as I come around him, my insides clenching against his shaft, pulsing and milking him as he hisses through his teeth. "Fuck, baby. Yes. Keep squeezing me." Then he hooks my leg over his shoulder picking up the pace, fingers gripping my hips as we collide, again and again and again. I don't come down, I just keep riding the high and howling with ecstasy, spiraling to yet another release.

"Nate!" I howl, my throat tearing as I scream.

"You feel too good, gorgeous. Just a little longer. I need to fuck you a little longer." Each word is punctuated with a thrust as he slams into me, skin slapping against skin. I might die if I don't come down soon, the pressure in my core is so intense that I may literally explode. *But what a way to go!*

"Oh, Nate! Fuuuuck!"

He grits his teeth as he buries himself deep with a bone-grinding pump. "Yes! *Delaney! Fuck!*" He shudders, and I scream, my entire body tightening and shaking. I honestly don't know which way is up or down anymore, and I have a feeling security will soon be knocking on our cabin door.

"Holy crap. Holy god. Holy Santa."

Nate's hand pushes my hair away from my face. "Holy Santa?" he asks, out of breath but smiling, his skin glistening with a sheen of sweat.

"Yeah. I prayed for a Christmas miracle, and it just came true," I gasp, smiling up at him because it's pretty much all I can do. *I'm ridiculously happy.*

"God, I love you," he says with a laugh as he gathers me up in his arms and carries me into the bathroom.

"I love you too. And I'm never going to get tired of saying that."

He nuzzles his nose against mine before he sets me on the ground then switches on the shower. "Me either. I love you, Delaney."

Grinning, I wrap my arms around his neck, kissing him as he steps us into the shower cubicle, the water sluicing over my exhausted but exhilarated body as we kiss and touch, and get ready to lose ourselves to the pleasure all over again. And as he picks me up and pins me against the tiled wall, entering me with a single thrust, I wonder how I ever lived without this. Nate is my perfect match, sent by the heavens to make my life complete. Now I just have to explain it to my family...

NATE

*D*elaney dozes in my arms, her soft body pressed into mine as her head rests against my chest. We've done nothing today except have sex and order room service. So, it's been the perfect day. There are about a thousand things to do on this cruise, but I think I'd be happy spending the rest of the ten days right here. *Delaney is mine.*

It feels like I've wanted her my entire life, even though I've only known her a short time. Ever since I moved back from LA, I've been searching for some sort of direction, a sign I made the right choice. I feel confident in saying my reason for turning my life upside down is asleep in my arms. Perfect and pure, and made just for me. It hits me pretty hard that I don't have a hell of a lot to offer her—no job, no prospects. All I have is my heart. I hope that's enough.

"What's got your brow all furrowed like that?" Delaney asks as she inhales and lifts her head, running a thumb over the creased lines between my eyebrows.

"I need a job."

She laughs slightly as she leans on my chest and looks at me properly. "That's what you're thinking about right now?"

"It is. I don't have one."

"Oh," she says, her expression shifting from amused to puzzled as she rolls onto her back. "Well...what were you planning to do when you left LA?"

"I have no idea. I kind of left on a whim. I was still trying to work out what options I had when Liz spoke to me about you."

"Oh. Well, I'll still pay you the rest of the money. We had an agreement and this doesn't change things," she says.

"I don't want you to, gorgeous. Seriously, I'm not here as an actor anymore. I'm here as your boyfriend, the man who loves you. Do not pay me for that." I meet her eyes, giving her a pointed look.

She blinks quickly. "OK. I won't."

"Thank you," I say, bringing her in close again,

my fingers stroking up and down her back as we lie together quietly.

"It doesn't bother me, you know."

"Well, it bothers me. A man should work. And I've never been out of work before."

"What are your skills?"

"Acting. That's literally all I've ever done."

"What about teaching? Have you thought about doing that? You could work in theater, in *schools*."

"I don't know," I sigh. "But I'll figure it out. I always do."

"Do you regret leaving?"

"LA?"

"Yeah."

"No. But I do regret the circumstances surrounding it."

"What do you mean?"

"My father had a lot to do with it, actually. And really, he's probably the reason I don't like Tony very much."

She lifts her head. "I'm listening."

"Well, my father had a habit of taking things that weren't his. Wallets, jewelry. Anything that wasn't nailed down properly. He also had a habit of stealing the limelight and thinking he was better than everyone. When I was younger, I'd be in plays and whatnot for school, and he'd always embarrass the crap out of me, turning up to rehearsals and trying to show everyone how it was done. To hear him tell it, he was just naturally better at everything than the rest of us. It was like in his eyes he was a God, but in everyone else's he was a drunk, and a failure. But he was still my father. And for all intents and purposes I loved him, even though I didn't particularly like him."

"I can understand that," she says. "I'm not blind to my parent's faults either—or Tony's."

"Last Thanksgiving, Dad came to LA to stay with me. I hadn't seen him in maybe five years. He'd been...*difficult* to get in contact with. Mom kept saying she thought he was in jail, but I don't know...it wouldn't have surprised me, though. Trouble just found the man, and I guess it was only a matter of time before it caught up. But that's neither here nor there at this point. The *point* is, it was just me and him for Thanksgiving, and I was working all the way through doing a bit part on a new Nickelodeon show. Things were going OK, and we were in talks about making my character a permanent fixture. But then my father decided to visit me on set. I don't know what he was on. But he was *lit*. He caused a scene, urinated in front of one of the kids, and to make a long story short, he got me kicked off set."

"Oh, no!" Delaney's eyes go wide, and I nod.

"I was this close," I say, holding my thumb and index finger about an inch apart. "I've had steady work for most of my career, but this was the first time I was on the cusp of having a permanent gig. Then Dad got involved and poof, it was all gone."

"I'm so sorry."

"We had a massive argument over it, and he left. By New Years, he had died"—Delaney gasps—"and that hit me pretty hard, but it was like he took my career into that grave with him. I was lucky if I could book a hemorrhoid cream commercial after that. His antics on set got me blackballed, and I was so angry with him that it was like I couldn't even mourn him properly. Then one day, after yet another failed audition, it all just hit me. My dad was gone, and we never got to say sorry, my career was in the toilet, and I was burning through my savings faster than I could add to them. I was going down, so something needed to change. I did the one thing that made sense to me, and I went back home. Mom lives in Florida now, but Burt and his wife were good enough to let me use their guest room to lick my wounds in. I literally present myself to you as a ruined man with no future except the one we make together. Now I'm just lying here trying to work out how I turn this all around. I mean, I've got the girl, right?"

"You've *definitely* got the girl."

I grin and press a kiss against her forehead. "So, that means all I have to do now is start a new career and get my own place. Should be easy, right?" I let out a sigh as I glance up to the ceiling. "I've been living in denial."

"Sounds to me like you've just been quietly mourning and coming to terms with your dad's passing, on top of his actions. It can't be easy losing someone after an argument, especially a parent. We all want to believe the best about them, no matter what behavior stares us in the face."

I take a deep breath and let it go as I turn to meet her eyes. "It did suck. I'm angry at him, but I still miss him, and I wish...I just wish things could've been different. But in the same breath, if none of that happened, I wouldn't be here with you right now. So despite the chaos, it all worked out for the best. And while you were sleeping, my own experience did get me to thinking, and I think maybe we should wait."

"Wait? I think it's a bit late now to wait for anything. We kind of did it all already..." She sits up, wraps the sheet around herself, and gives me a look of confusion that just makes me smile. "I mean, I'm sure there's *plenty* more *positions and techniques*. But for the sake of things we could wait for...there isn't a lot left." She pauses and looks at me properly, tilting her head in question. "Wait. Why are you laughing at me?"

"Because you're adorable, sexy, innocent,

quirky, and every positive adjective I can think of to describe you." I sit up and move closer to her and slide my hands around her waist, dropping a gentle kiss on the end of her nose.

"I think we can both attest to the fact that I'm not so innocent anymore," she says with a cheeky little smirk.

"No, gorgeous. You're deliciously dirty, and my dick is getting hard just thinking about being back inside you. But before I hold you down on the bed and fuck you till you're screaming again, I need to finish saying that I think we should wait until *after* the cruise to tell your family Liam doesn't exist."

"What do you mean? I thought this is what you wanted."

"It is. But I've also done a little soul-searching here, and I realize that it's a bit of a selfish thing for me to ask of you. Especially this close to Christmas, and *especially* on a cruise that's all about your family. If we do this now, we could cause a rift, or at least a hell of a lot of drama. And out of all of your family, your Aunty is probably my favorite person—besides you, of course— and I don't want to be responsible for ruining her big event. She obviously went to a lot of trouble to set this up for you all. And I don't think it hurts either of us to play along for a few more days. We can let everyone know the truth behind our meeting in the new year."

"Do you really mean that?"

"I do. The one thing I know for sure is that I am hopelessly in love with you. You can call me Liam or you can call me Nate, and that fact isn't going to change. So, for the sake of keeping the peace for the holidays, and maybe vicariously repairing the messed up holidays I experienced last year, I can handle pretending a little longer. But only with them, I don't want to do any pretending with you."

"I could never pretend about how I feel toward you, Nate. You have my heart and you always will. I honestly think I was born loving you."

"Yeah?" I lean in close and brush my lips against hers. "I have a feeling I was born to love you too."

"Have I mentioned how much I love you today?" she asks as she runs her fingers down my chest.

"You have. But I'd like to hear it again."

"I love you, Nate."

"Music to my ears." I lean down and kiss her swollen lips, my tongue seeking hers as we lean back against the bed. Just as my dick is good and ready for another round of 'Watch Delaney come then fuck her senseless' there's a knock at the door.

"Go away!" we both call out at the same time. Delaney giggles as a voice calls through the door.

"We're all going to the waterslides and Mom said to drag you along too." The voice seems to belong to Tommy, so I groan as I pull back from Delaney and grab a towel to secure around my waist as I make my way to the door.

"Raincheck?" I say as I pull the door open slightly. "We kind of have our own game going on here."

I lift my brow as Tommy nods knowingly, then Tony—who I didn't realize was in attendance—bursts in through the door. "You two are into water sports? Eww." He goes straight to our mini bar and takes the replenished bourbon bottles, downing two of them straight away.

"Tony! Get out!" Delaney yells from where she remains covered on the bed.

"What are you gonna do? Tell Mom?" he sneers.

"I'll tell your *wife*," Delaney snaps back, and Tony's mouth drops open with an expression that reads as, 'You wouldn't!'.

"Come on, man. Let's give them the chance to get dressed," Tommy says as Delaney pokes her tongue out at Tony and throws a pillow his way. It makes him drop some of the goodies he took from our fridge, so he scrambles to pick them up before rushing out the door. Tommy rolls his eyes. "He's always been the unkempt one. We'll see you two on deck?"

"Sure. We'll be there in twenty minutes," I say before chaining the door and turning back to my gorgeous girl. "Actually, let's make that an hour. I need one more round with that delicious body of yours before I'm ready to face the real world again."

"I like the way you think." She giggles as I whip off my towel and dive on the bed to ravish her.

DELANEY

"Everybody say cheese!" Aunty Joan says as one of the staff members take a family photo of us all standing next to the massive water slides. The kids are all kneeled down in front, and the adults are lined up behind.

"Cheese!" We chorus as the young man takes a few rapid photos before handing Aunty Joan her cellphone back.

"Thank you so much, young man," she says, slipping him a tip as she peruses the images on her phone. "These are just great. I'm going to get them printed up and mail them out to all of you so we can all have a copy." She nods, feeling very proud of that idea.

"You don't have to *print* the photos, Aunty," I point out. "You can just send us a digital copy, and we'll all get to keep it in our photo albums."

"Well, that's why I want to print it," she replies. "For your photo albums."

"What Delaney's trying to say," Nate starts, "is that we all have digital photo albums on our cellphones. So if you email or text the photos to all of our cells, we'll get to save it and carry it around with us everywhere."

"Oh. Well, how do I do that?" She hands him her phone, and he talks her through it, making my heart swell with pride because my man is seriously so patient and caring. Whether he's acting as Liam or as himself, he is a genuinely good person. Not everyone has the fortitude to explain technology to an old woman. But he stands there with her and talks her through each step until she's happily doing it herself.

"What is he doing?" Mom asks, moving up beside me as I watch Nate and Aunty Joan.

"He's showing her how to send photos to people," I say, noting the way her eyes widen at the thought.

"My god. Why would he do such a thing? She'll never stop. Have you any idea how many photos that woman actually takes? It's mind-numbing. I've had to upgrade her cloud storage three times this year to free up space on her cell. And I blame Tommy for that, he's the one who bought her the iPhone photography book for Christmas last year."

"What's the harm if she's having fun?" I ask, still smiling.

"Oh, you'll see," Mom says as she steps away. "And don't say I didn't warn you."

It's at that moment my phone starts blowing up, message after message coming through. The first contains the family portrait, then there are a few more images of us all on the cruise, and the final one is a picture of Nate and me last night. We're walking away from her, his hand about my waist as he leans down to say something in my ear. It looks so beautiful. A tiny window into the love that was building between us before we even spoke about it out loud.

Lifting my eyes from the screen, I find Nate watching me, his gaze soft and heated. I place my hand on my heart to show him how touched I am by the image, and even though we just taught Aunty Joan that you don't need to print photos out anymore, this one is particular, is definitely going to hard copy. I want it on my wall so I can see this moment always.

"Prepare for an onslaught of pictures. She's just getting started," Nate says as he returns to my side and draws me in close, pressing a soft kiss to my lips before bringing his mouth to my ear and speaking so only I can hear. "Think I can take you back to the cabin and continue playing our own version of slip and slide yet?"

"I think we might have to stick around here a little longer," I say, grinning as my phone buzzes in my hand again. It's a photo of Nate and me kissing just now. "Thank you, Aunty."

She waves a hand over her head from her position seated under a shade umbrella. "And thank you! Seeing you two so in love makes this old woman happy. Now go and have some fun. I'm happy right here taking my pictures."

Leaving my bag near her seat, Nate and I head off hand in hand in search of my brothers and their kids. Lucy and Tarryn are at the bar with Mom and Dad, ordering a round of fruity cocktails by the look of it, but Tommy and Tony are kid wrangling—not because they have to, but because they were desperate to have a turn on the water slides too. I'm torn between wanting the cocktail and wanting to have fun. It's been a very long time since I've been brave enough to go down one of these things. Body issues tend to keep me poolside with a sarong covering my non-desirable bits. But after the way this big muscular man beside me has been worshipping my oversized body, I'm feeling rather...sexy I have to admit. And I know, I shouldn't base my body confidence on what a man thinks about me, but it's genuinely hard not to. We get told to be one way or another all our lives so we're constantly critical of what we see in our reflection. But when someone who you find beautiful finds you beautiful too...well, that reflection is suddenly a hell of a lot better, as if they somehow managed to lend you their eyes so you can feel as attractive as they find you. It's a heady drug.

"Looks like there are three slides to choose from," Nate says as we make our way to the entry point. "Slow to fast. Where would you like to start?"

"It's been so long since I've been on one. So probably the one in the middle?" I suggest, loving the feel of his fingers laced between mine. I'd also be happy to just stand around like this all day, smiling up at him and acting all ga-ga. I've never been in love before, so having this—having *him*—is a novelty.

"OK. Let's show these kids how it's done."

We spend the next few hours lining up and sliding down, spending quality time with my nieces and nephews as well as my brothers. When Tommy and Tony are both together, they're a riot. They feed off each other's energy, and Tommy becomes more boisterous while Tony because less...*Tony*. The kids think Nate is king and take turns going down the slide with him, or just hanging from his shoulders. And somehow, I fall a little harder with every moment that passes. There's something about seeing a mammoth of a man being gentle with children that just turns you to mush.

"You seem happy," Tommy says as I take a breather, waiting for Nate to pop out the end of the slide with Tommy's boy Cory.

"I am. I'm really happy," I say, laughing as they both pop out, water spraying up in their faces before they come to a stop.

"Good. I'm happy for you. And Nathaniel. You both seem a lot more at ease than you were at Thanksgiving."

"We are," I say with a smile before I freeze, icy fingers trailing a line down my spine. "Wh-what did you just call him?"

"Nathaniel. That's his name, right?"

"Ah..." *Ohmygod,ohmygod,ohmygod.*

"It's OK." His eyes swing to meet mine. "I get it. There's been a lot of shitty pressure on you from the parentals to settle down. I'm just happy to see you happy for a change. Those guys they kept pushing you to date were the worst."

"Wait. I'm lost. Ho-how do you know his name?" My face is flaming and I feel like I might vomit. No one was supposed to find us out until we were ready to tell them.

"I've seen him on TV. Tarryn's a big Law & Order fan. He played a wrongly accused murderer."

My mouth opens, but I just don't know what

to say. Sure, Nate and I were going to tell everyone the truth in the New Year. But it's an entirely different thing to have someone blatantly tell you they knew all along. "Who else knows?" I whisper, finally getting some words out.

"No one. Just me. And if Tarryn has twigged, she hasn't said."

"Ah..."

"It's OK, Del. I'm not telling anyone. I actually think it was an ingenious plan from the get-go. Hire a guy to get them off your back then say you broke up sometime later. Perfect. But I'm more happy that you found a connection with him. Not sure how you're going to broach it with the oldies, but, really, does it matter what they think?"

"I, ah...Does Nate know about this?" I ask, my head spinning. I really never imagined a scenario where anyone would actually recognize Nate from his work.

"Does he know that I know?" He frowns. "Well, yeah. I spoke to him about it at Thanksgiving. He didn't tell you?"

"No," I whisper. I don't know how I feel about this. Especially when a big part about why Nate *didn't* want to take this next step was dependent on me being willing to come clean. You'd think he'd use the fact that Tommy already knows in his favor. On top of that, telling me would have saved me a hell of a lot of embarrassment right now. I actually feel foolish, exposed. I didn't want anyone knowing until I was ready to tell.

"Don't be too hard on him. Like I said, I was never going to tell. I guess he just didn't want you feeling worried or uncomfortable."

"Sure," I say, offering him a fake smile as I force my face into a mask of composure. "I'm sure that's all that was behind it."

"What's happening?" Nate says as he walks over with Tony and the kids. The older of the four, Anna and Mitchell are talking about wanting to go on the bigger, faster slide.

"Why don't we meet you there?" I say to my brothers.

"Sorry, buddy," Tommy says, offering a tight-lipped smile as he heads off with Tony who's asking if something happened while Nate turns to me and wants to know the same thing.

"Am I missing something?"

"Why didn't you tell me Tommy knows who you are?" I hiss, my annoyance flaring as I meet his eyes.

His mouth opens then closes. But ultimately, he just shakes his head. "I don't know. I guess...I guess I trusted him to keep it to himself. And since we're telling everyone soon, anyway, I really didn't think it mattered."

"Of course it matters. Tony and Tommy are

twins. They tell each other *everything*. And Tony... he won't keep it to himself."

"I really don't think that's the case, Delaney. There seems to be quite a few things that Tommy and Tony aren't on the same page about. I honestly think we're safe here. And it's just until the new year." He reaches out and places his hands on my hips, bringing me in closer so he can nuzzle my neck. "Once everyone knows, it'll just be you and me and this body of yours making sweet, sweet love for the rest of our lives." I actually melt.

"Gosh, you're right. You're right. I'm overreacting. I just wasn't expecting to feel so outed on the first day I'm feeling truly happy."

"Is that because I make you happy?"

"You make me *very* happy," I say, threading my fingers through his damp hair as I hold tight to him. "And I think I've had enough family time now. Let's make excuses and go back to our cabin."

"I don't think we need to make excuses," he says, pulling back slightly so his deep blue eyes meet mine. "If there's anything I want to be painfully honest about, it's the way I feel about you. So I say we just go over there and get your bag, and tell them we're taking the rest of the day for ourselves."

"And what about dinner? We're supposed to

meet them all for dinner and a show. It's some magician tonight. One of the guys who fooled Penn and Teller."

"Sounds crazy exciting. But do you know what I think is even better? Room service and fucking. Think you can handle more of that?"

"I might not walk straight tomorrow, but hell yeah," I say with a naughty grin. "Room service and fucking sounds like a hell of a lot more fun."

NATE

"Hmm." Delaney hums against my mouth as my fingers move inside her. In and out, in and out, while we sit in the middle of the bed facing each other.

"Feel good?"

"Mmm-hmmm."

Adding my thumb into the mix, I tease her clit and kiss her with languid movement, my tongue moving in time with my fingers. Her hips rock against my hands, her whimpers becoming deeper then higher as I bring her to the brink then tease her right back down again.

"Oh, Nate, please."

"Soon, gorgeous. Soon. I'm enjoying taking my time with you. I like watching you come, but I love that moment just *before* you come. The way your body tightens and heats beneath my touch.

Sometimes that's all I want to see, so I'm going to tease you and tease you until your body just can't come back anymore."

"Hmm. Remind me to return the favor sometime," she murmurs as she releases a needy sigh.

"You *really* want me to make you come, huh?" I chuckle before I lean in and gently suck on her bottom lip.

"I do," she pants. "I really, really do."

"Sit on my lap," I instruct, watching the way her eyes flick down to my erect cock, and she licks her lips.

"I get to ride you?"

"Yeah." I wrap my hand around her back and hold my dick steady. "I want you to sit *right* here and show me how badly you want to come."

"OK."

She lets out a moan as she lowers herself over my shaft, taking me deep inside, my shaft surrounded by her wet heat. With all the touching and teasing, I've worked myself into a frenzy, and it only takes a few grinds of her pelvis against mine to have me hissing through my teeth.

"Uh-ah. Not yet," she whispers, raking her teeth over my stubbled chin as her arms wrap around my shoulders. "I want to see that moment *before* you come."

I chuckle as I place my hands on her hips, my

fingers digging into her flesh. "Touché," I say as I look into her lust-filled eyes. "But I've got something up my sleeve you don't."

"What's that?"

Pushing up onto my knees, I flip her onto her back, keeping myself inside her so I regain control of our movement. "I've got strength."

She moans as I thrust my hips, burying myself with force. "Who's to say this isn't exactly what I wanted."

I'm caught between a laugh and a moan as she claws at my chest and arms before she slides her hands around to my back, pressing her fingers into my skin as I thrust and thrust, pumping back and forth with increasing speed, her cries growing lower as the friction builds, spiraling us both toward our combined crescendo. She throws her head back, howling as her insides tighten around me when her orgasm tears through her body. Mine is quick to follow, hard, fast, and hot, spilling into her body as I bury myself and still, my chest heaving from the exertion.

"That was intense," I pant, my forehead touching against hers as we slowly catch our breath and come back down to earth from our combined high.

"Was it ever. I take back all the whining. That was worth every bit of teasing."

I chuckle as I gather her up in my arms and

carry her to the bathroom, something that's quickly become a tradition between us—make love, clean up, make love, and get dirty all over again. In the last few days, it's been our primary activity on the cruise. Not the on-deck entertainment, the shopping or the shows. No, the only thing of true interest is right here in this room.

"Two more nights and then we're back in San Francisco," Delaney says with a sigh as she runs a straightening iron through her hair to get ready for dinner. Tonight is Christmas Eve, so it's an extra special evening for her family. They observe the Icelandic tradition of Jolabokaflod, which is the act of giving each other books on Christmas Eve. I was aware of this tradition from the info folder Delaney gave me when she hired me. So I spent over an hour in the bookstore trying to decide what I want to give her. I wanted the book to hold meaning, but at the time, I wasn't aware of her fiction likes and dislikes, so I found myself looking for books about inspirational women who forged their own path the way Delaney has hers. I settled on a book about Coco Chanel, and since it caught my eye, I got her a second book called 'You are a Badass'. It's all about following your own path and remembering that you call the shots in your world. When I bought it, I thought it was exactly the kind of book Delaney needed. But now I'm not so sure. Over the last few days, we've had various discussions about her family and the roles they play in her life, and I think she sees them for what they are, but because she loves them, she looks past all of those faults and cares for them anyway. My opinion now is that we should all be so kind and caring. The world needs more Delaney's.

"I've loved every moment with you on this cruise, but I'm really keen to get back home and get my life moving," I say as I slide the books out of the side compartment of my bag and try to decide whether I should give her one or both. I'm thankful I brought a gift bag to put them in or I'd be stuck with them wrapped together.

"I have every confidence you'll find your feet," she says from inside the bathroom. "And in the meantime, I was thinking that maybe you'd be interested in being the face of our men's skincare range. We're not far off launching..." Her voice grows louder as she approaches so I make a quick decision and drop the Coco Chanel book in the gift bag and dump the Bad Ass one back in my bag. Except it misses and lands at my feet. Just as she rounds the doorway. "And it won't be a huge amount of work, but I think you're exactly the right—" She freezes as her eyes drop to the book at my feet, and a smile crosses her features. "Is that for me?"

Before she can lean down to pick it up, I squat

down to snatch it off the ground. But before I can stand back up and hide it, we collide, our foreheads bumping hard enough to make the back of my eyes hurt and knock poor Delaney on her ass. "Crap. Shit. I'm so sorry," I say, holding out my hand to help her up.

"Now I really want to see that book," she moans, rubbing her head as I pull her back to standing. "It must be interesting if you're willing to headbutt me for it."

"You took it like a champ," I say with a chuckle as I cradle her face in my palm and check that there isn't any swelling. There's a red mark, but it looks like she's come out of it relatively unscathed.

"Hand over the book, Mister." She looks up at me with that no-nonsense expression in her eyes that I'm already coming to admire. It's the special something she has that I believe is the attitude behind her ability to break into an already flooded market.

"Fine. But for the record, I bought you two books because I wasn't sure what you'd like. This is the one I chose *not* to give you."

"You Are a Badass: How to Stop Doubting Your Greatness and Start Living an Awesome Life," she reads from the bright yellow cover as I place it in her palm then looks up to meet my eyes. "You think I doubt my greatness?"

"I did. But now I think you know exactly what you're doing, which is why I was officially giving you a different book. Please don't be offended."

"I'm not," she says, smiling as she turns the book over and reads the back. "Because I love this. I love that you put so much thought into something when you barely even knew me. And I do need this in my life. I doubt myself *all* the time. It's perfect. Thank you." She leans up and kisses me with her plum-painted lips. "Want to know what book I bought you?"

"Of course."

She presses her lips together then moves over to her side of the closet and pulls open a drawer. "When I bought this, I did it knowing that you had just let go of a dream. So I chose this out of compassion. I've also been nervous about giving it to you, but I don't have a backup book so..." She takes out a beautifully wrapped package and hands it to me.

"Shouldn't I be waiting until after dinner to do this with the family?"

"No," she says with a tiny head shake. "I think this is something better opened away from prying eyes."

"Is it a guide to using fleshlights?"

She giggles. "*No*. Just open it."

"OK." I slide my thumb along the seam and pop the tape, carefully removing the paper from the book before turning it over and studying the hardback cover. "Man's Search for Meaning." I lift my eyes to meet hers as she wrings her fingers together.

"At first, I thought it was too much. It's about how humans need to find meaning in any given situation, no matter how bleak. I thought it might give you some perspective to help you figure out where you want to go in life outside of LA. But after finding out about your father and the *reason* you walked away, I think it's the perfect text to show you that there's always a path to where you want to go. It might just look different from how you originally imagined it." A lump forms in my throat as I read the back of the book then set it to the side. "You hate it. Don't you?"

"No," I whisper, taking her face in my hands. "I think it's thoughtful and perfect. Just like you." Her expression softens as I bring my mouth to hers, kissing her slow and true until our breathing picks up and our bodies press in close. Before I know it, I have her dress up about her waist and I'm lifting her against the closet wall, lining myself up with her entrance before plunging inside her. "I'm so in love with you, Delaney Gilchrist."

"And I'm so in love with you, Nate Charmers," she gasps between thrusts. And I marvel at just how intense the connection we have truly is. I've never felt this way about anyone. I can't wait to go home and start the rest of my life with her.

～

"Milady," I say, grinning as I hold Delaney's chair out for her. We're in a private dining room tonight, skipping the buffets and crowds for something more intimate. It reminds me a lot of Thanksgiving, which also gives me the warm fuzzies since that's the day I lost my heart and Delaney found it. Sure, we had our issues getting to this happy point, but as I take my seat beside her at this festive feast, I press a kiss to her shoulder and feel grateful for every moment we experienced getting here. I feel like it only brought us closer sooner.

"If I can make a toast," Joan says as she stands at the head of the table with her champagne glass lifted in the air. "I want to thank you all for taking time out of your busy schedules to be here. I know it wasn't easy to organize time away from work and school, but you all managed it, and this old lady is eternally grateful to you for making this year the most special Christmas yet. I do so love our holiday time together, and I know you're all worried about my health, but I assure you, I'm not dying—not that I know of, anyway. But I do have some bone density issues, and just general ninety-five-year-old lady tiredness that have made me realize that I won't be so sprightly forever. I wanted to have one fantastic trip with those I love most before I retire to my estate and hire male strippers to clean my house and wait on me as entertainment." There's a titter around the room, but I have a feeling she might be serious. "So with that in mind, I'd like you all to raise your glasses as I wish you a very merry Christmas. I hope Santa is kind to you all in the morning."

"Merry Christmas," we chorus, raising our glasses as the first course of stuffed mushrooms is brought into the room and placed in front of us.

"Now, let's feast," she says, rubbing her hands together as she takes her seat and lifts her cutlery.

"I was wondering if I might say something," Tony asks as he taps his glass and stands, not waiting for an answer. Joan graciously gestures for him to go ahead, nonetheless. "Thank you. First off, I think I can speak for all of us when I say that this cruise has been a magnificent gift, Aunty, and I thank you from the bottom of my heart. It's brought us all closer in ways I couldn't imagine. And it's also revealed a few...*truths* about the people in our midst." His gaze lands on me. *Uh-oh.* "Now, I know we normally do the book gifting thing at the end of dinner. But I happen to have uncovered some reading material I think we'd all like to get stuck into immediately." He pulls a stack of photocopies from a gift bag and passes them around the table. Delaney and I look at each other with concern. *Double uh-oh.*

It's a triple uh-oh by the time the papers get to us because staring right at me is Delaney's familiar handwriting on the front page. It's a copy of the script changes she made earlier in the week, stapled to all the information she gave me at the coffee house. *How the hell does he have this?* It should have been safely inside my folder, *inside* my bag, *inside* our closet. He's been snooping...

"Where did you get this?" Delaney demands, her eyes flashing with fire as she flips the pages.

"I think the more important question here is why does this exist?" Tony says, waving the copies in accusation just as their father looks up in confusion.

"What the hell were you doing going through my things?" I snap.

"I found the first part on the floor," Tony returns, while I'm picturing myself jumping across the table to wipe the smug look off his face.

"What am I even looking at here?" Roger asks, trying to get some sort of explanation out of the tense room.

Delaney shakes her head, her eyes brimming as she looks at me for a way out. But there isn't one. We can't undo this. Tony has outed us, and there's no other way to explain this except to admit that we lied.

"Delaney," her mother says as she flicks through the pages. "Is all of this true?"

"It's true, Gladys," I admit, meeting her eyes as her mouth gapes and she grabs onto her husband's hand for support.

"Where did this even come from?" Joan asks, scrutinizing it in a business-like manner that has me thinking that's exactly how she became as successful as she is.

"Our cabin," I inform her, placing my hand over Delaney's as she turns a bright shade of red and seems to shrink back into her chair. "It was tucked away in my luggage, actually." I let my eyes fall on Tony who's just looking self-satisfied. Then they move to Tommy who shakes his head at me, as if saying this wasn't him. *I hope that's true.* I'd hate to think I trusted him only to have this come out of it. My anger isn't even about me. It's about a brother doing something to purposefully call out his sister.

"And what is it, exactly?" Joan asks, bringing my attention back to her. "I know what it *looks* like. But I'd like to hear it from you."

"When Delaney and I first met, it was to hire me to play her boyfriend for the holidays," I say.

"To *play* her boyfriend?" Gladys balks. "What does that even mean?"

"It means that he's an actor, Mom," Tony says, a look of sheer delight in his beady eyes. "Delaney has been lying to us this whole time. They're pretending to be together just so they can trick Aunty Joan."

"But why? I don't understand." Gladys blusters.

"Explain yourself, young lady," Roger booms.

"I..." Delaney blinks rapidly, trying to keep her tears at bay, but can't even get the words out. This isn't how it was supposed to go down.

"She did it because you people won't get off her back," I snap, refusing to sit here and listen to them attack her like this is her fault. As far as I'm concerned, they pushed her to this point, and her brother should be the one who's getting questioned over being an insidious asshole. "Just because she was single doesn't mean she needed to be set up with every random guy you thrust at her. She was perfectly capable of choosing a man for herself. And she did. She chose me."

"I have no idea what's going on," Tarryn mutters, picking up her champagne glass and signaling for a refill. Our poor waiter—who's incidentally doing a wonderful job of pretending not to hear the drama unfolding in front of him—scuttles over and tops her off, probably relieved to have something to do.

"Liam is an actor," Lucy says. "Remember that

episode of Law & Order where the guy is wrongly accused of murder and is almost killed in prison? That's him."

Tarryn's eyes go wide as she slurps at her drink. "I *thought* he looked familiar."

"Ohmigod," Delaney gasps, sinking lower in her chair. "Kill me now. This *isn't* happening."

"Yes, I'm an actor," I say. "I've been a small part actor for most of my adult life. But I think you're missing the point here—regardless of *why* we met, Delaney and I *are* actually dating. We fell for each other right at the start."

"Wait. So your real name *is* Liam?" Gladys asks.

"His name is Nathaniel Charmers," Tony puts in.

"I prefer to be called Nate," I say, trying to keep track of the conversation. "But my name doesn't change the fact that I'm in love with—"

"Lying!" Tony yells over me. "You came into our lives and blatantly lied about who and what you are—you're no *dentist*—and what makes things worse is that our sister is the one who put you up to it! She lied to you, Aunty Joan. Took advantage of your generosity by faking a relationship just to stay in your good graces—we all know you love being the favorite, Delaney—and if I were you, Aunty Joan, I'd feel so used that I'd cut her off altogether. She doesn't deserve to be rewarded for her duplicity."

"What did I ever do to you?" Delaney yells as tears stream down her face. "Why would you do this to purposely embarrass me at Christmas?"

"Your little stunt made you embarrass yourself, Delaney. I just brought it out into the open."

"That's quite enough!" Joan yells as more voices get thrown into the mix and the noise escalates. Her volume is quite impressive for her stature. "Shame on you. Both of you." She presses her lips together and looks between Tony and Delaney. "Shame on you, Delaney, for thinking you could lie to us and we wouldn't find out. And shame on you, Tony, for embarrassing your sister and ruining a family tradition with your jealousy and callousness. How dare you even *suggest* what *I* should do with *my* money. Don't think I'm unaware of those dollar signs in your eyes, young man. But the joke's on you. You have no idea who or what is in my will."

I can't help but notice Tommy smirking, and it seems Joan doesn't miss it either. "Do you want to tell them or should I?" she asks him with a conspiratorial smile.

Pushing his sleeves higher up his arms, Tommy straightens in his seat. "Oh, can I?"

Joan lifts her hand in a flutter. "Go ahead. Let's put the record straight once and for all," she says as she picks up her champagne glass and drinks while Tommy informs the family that none of them are in the will and all of Aunty Joan's estate is going to charity when she dies. I don't get a chance to see anyone's reaction, though, because Delaney is quick to take that moment of stunned silence to slip from the room, and I don't waste any time in following her.

"Delaney," I call out, rushing to catch up with her. "Are you OK?"

"I'm humiliated," she sniffs, hitting the button for the elevator that will take us to our cabin. "Tony *stole* that from our cabin and *humiliated* me with it. Why? What'd I ever do to him?"

"I don't know, baby." The elevator arrives, and I wrap my arms around her as we step inside, enveloped in jaunty Christmas music as we make the climb to our floor. "Maybe he's jealous of how close you and your aunt are? Or maybe he resents you for leaving and starting your own life without them? He comes across as a bit of a curmudgeon to me, so maybe he just enjoys being a dick."

"Probably," she sniffs as the doors open and we're presented with our floor. "God, I hate that tonight was ruined because of this. We were supposed to have a nice meal and feel all Christ-massy after we gave each other our books."

"Hey, none of that was your fault, OK? Tony did that all by himself. There were probably a hundred different ways he could have handled that, and he chose to do it in the most selfish and dramatic way possible. That's *not* on you."

"I know, I just…I just hate feeling like this."

"I know, gorgeous," I say as I let us into our cabin then just draw her into my arms, holding her tight as she cries. "Silver lining is that we were going to tell them soon anyway. My only real regret tonight is not sticking around to see the look on Tony's face when he realized your aunt won't be leaving him any money."

"You're right. That would have been kind of funny. He's got himself mortgaged to the hilt thinking he's going to inherit. So, I guess it kind of serves him right for spending money he doesn't have." She smiles for a millisecond before she frowns. "Actually, that makes me feel sad too. This whole thing does. I feel bad for Aunty Joan. It must feel awful knowing people are looking at you for what you can give them when you die."

"I have a feeling your Aunty Joan knew exactly what was going on in everyone's head. I think she took great delight in bursting their greed bubbles tonight."

She leans into my shoulder with a sigh. "I kind of hope she does pay male strippers to do her housework once we go back home. I think that would be hilarious."

"Me too, gorgeous. Me too." I press a kiss to

the top of her head, enjoying just holding her like this, quiet and still. I get to thinking about our future, about creating Christmas traditions of our own once we have kids. I'd enjoy reading them stories by the fireplace on Christmas Eve and knowing that no matter what path they choose in life, Delaney and I will always have their backs. They'll be none of this expectation, taking over, or put-downs that we've seen inside our own families. No, Delaney and I will start fresh with a clean slate. Together, we've got this.

I'm just about to communicate all of this to her when there's a knock at our door.

"Tell them to go away," she says, making me smile because I remember issuing a similar request only a few days ago.

"It might be your aunty or Tommy," I say. "We still like them, right?"

"I suppose," she pouts, leaning against the back of the couch as I get up to answer the door. Joan bursts in with two staff members carrying a small Christmas tree and a Santa sack. Joan also has a pink sparkly Santa hat on her head. She looks very festive with her white hair poking out and her painted lips slashing across her face in a bright smile.

"Ho, ho, ho!" she says, her smile wide as the staff set the tree and the bag of gifts to the side of the room. "Normally Santa likes to wait until you're sleeping to deliver gifts, but I thought you could do with a pick me up a little sooner. No peeking until the morning though." She waggles a finger at us both before turning her smiling face to me. "And if you could give us a quiet moment, Nathaniel, I'd like to have a chat with my niece."

"Oh, of course. I...I'll go take a walk," I say, pointing out the door the staff just exited.

"Wonderful," she says, her hands clasped together. "But don't go too far. I'd like to speak to you too."

"Me?"

"You did say you're in love with my niece, didn't you?"

"I am, I—"

"Then I want to talk to you." She smiles and tilts her head, and I'm not sure what to think.

"I guess I'll be back in fifteen minutes?"

"Make it ten," she says. "And Nate?"

"Yes?" I pause in the doorway and meet her eyes. "I watch Law & Order too."

DELANEY

"Oh, what a mess that turned out to be," Aunty Joan says as she lowers herself onto the couch next to me with a groan before she turns my way, smiles, and sighs.

"I'm so sorry, Aunty Joan. I—"

"For what? Nathaniel was right. We *have* been pushing men at you. I've been so blinded by my own regrets that I stuck my nose in where it wasn't wanted. And I made you uncomfortable. For that, I'm sorry."

"It's OK. I know you were only doing it out of concern. I just…I couldn't keep pretending to like these men anymore. So, I invented one of my own. I'm sorry for deceiving you."

"Oh gosh, you didn't deceive me at all. I watch so much TV that I recognized him straight away. He's obviously much more famous than he thinks he is. As Lucy mentioned, he's been on Law & Order, and I've seen him in Grey's Anatomy—I'm fairly sure I spotted him in an episode of Modern Family—and that's not to mention all the movies he's been in. I mentioned thinking he was an actor to Tommy after Thanksgiving and he and I went through his IMDB page, and I have to say I'm so impressed. So many speaking roles. Whatever is he doing taking a fake boyfriend role that involves no acting credit?"

"His father passed away, and they didn't finish up on good terms," I say, and she nods, a knowing expression on her face.

"Oh, grief mixed with regret is a powerful tool for change. And, again, I'm sorry for trying to right my own remorse by pushing my agenda onto you. I suppose I did it because I see so much of myself in you, dear. You have that same tenacity I had, the get-up and go, the fight inside you to bend the world and shape it to your will...it's so special to see that in you. But I also know that once the work and the drive aren't there anymore, you look around and realize it's very lonely at the top. I kept telling myself that I still had time, that I could have love and family *later,* always later. But I left it too long, and my time was up." She releases a heavy breath and gives me a rueful smile. "I see you, pet. And I know that you are going to be an amazing success. I'm so proud of everything you've done so far, especially because you did it all by yourself—which is a little more than I can say for the rest of them. But, I digress. My point is, I wanted you to find love before you got caught up in chasing success. That way, you'd know the man you love, loves you for you and not your money or your connections. It becomes very difficult to know who to trust and what their intentions are. Even your own family can be a little dubious at times. But at least with family, I understand their intention a little clearer. Still, it can be very hard to know who to trust."

"I'm sorry, Aunty Joan. I knew you had regrets about not getting married and having kids, but I didn't understand that struggle quite as much as I do right now. And if it's any consolation, I never looked at you for your money. I just thought you were fun and amazing, and I always wanted to be like you."

"Oh, I know, sweet girl. That's why you've always been my obvious favorite and why your brother thought he needed to discredit you like that. He had it in his head that I'd leave everything to you since I make it quite obvious that I like you so much. But, we set *that* record straight just now, and he can go back to his room and lick his wounds until tomorrow morning when he'll be required to eat his words and grovel once he realizes what the surprise I have for you all is. I love the boy, but my gosh, he's always been a greedy little shit. He should have been a bank manager just so he could go and sit in the vault and smell the money for fun."

I let out a giggle as I wipe my hands under my eyes, patting away all of my half-dried tears. "So you're really not angry with me?" I ask. "For making Liam up and hiring Nate to play him?"

"No. Not at all. At first, I admit I was... confused. But Tommy pointed out that your mother and I have put a little too much focus on your marital status over the years. Plus, I could see how enamored you both were with each other. And I know I'm not supposed to print all of those pictures up, but I couldn't help myself." She turns away from me as she digs around in her bag. "You know, there's a little store on the ship that makes photo books. So, I had them make a little love story in pictures from all the happy snaps I took of you both since Thanksgiving. Sometimes, I think it helps us to see ourselves how other people see us. And this is how I see you—happy and in love." She pulls a wrapped square from her bag and hands it to me. "Happy Jolabokaflod."

"Oh, Aunty Joan. This is so incredibly thoughtful," I say as I tear open the paper and run my hand over the front cover. It's a glossy image of Nate and me kissing at the waterslides.

When I open the book, there's a chronicle of secretly caught moments of us together, smiling, touching, gazing…I just love it, and I will treasure it always. "Thank you."

"You're so welcome," she says with a happy sigh as she pats me on the knee. "Now, if you can take a short walk and possibly go and speak to your mother, then I'll get that dashing man of yours in here and have a talk with him. Do you think you can do that for an old woman who loves you, dear?"

With a laugh, I lean in and embrace her. "Of course, Aunty Joan. Anything for you. And thank you again—for this talk, for understanding, and for the beautiful book."

"Always. You'll find your mother in the bar drinking daiquiris. She's having a meltdown." Aunty Joan is smirking when I turn back to her, and I sigh before heading for the door, resigned to having a much more difficult conversation with my mother than the one I just had with Aunty Joan. *Maybe I should get Tommy to soften Mom too?*

"She's ready for you," I say as I step into the hall and find Nate leaning against the opposite wall.

"Are we in shit?" he asks, his worried eyes meeting mine.

I shake my head and move toward him, sliding my arms around his waist. "Seems she's a bit of a fan of yours, actually. I don't think you and I really fooled anyone."

"Not even each other." He smiles as he bows his head and brushes his nose against mine. "I was head over heels for you the moment you tapped my shoulder in that coffee house."

"And I couldn't believe my lucky stars when I saw you. I thought, if I have to pay to have a boyfriend, please let him be this guy. And it was, and I'm so happy that this turned into something more. So, no matter how dramatic my mom is over this, I'll never regret it for a moment because otherwise I would never have met you. You have my heart, Nate Charmers. And I never want you to give it back."

Grinning, he touches his lips to mine before deepening the kiss and holding me tight, making me feel like I've won the boyfriend lottery. "I love you, Delaney," he whispers as he releases me.

"I love you too," I return, pressing my lips to his once more before I step back and gesture toward our cabin. "And good luck in there. She might be a sweet little lady most of the time, but she's got a sharp tongue when she wants to."

"I've no doubt," Nate says. "Where are you off to now?"

"Mom's in the bar drinking up a storm. Seems I've driven her to drink."

"I'll meet you up there after?"

"No. Wait for me here. I want to spend the rest of the night alone with you. No family. No drama. No clothes."

He chuckles as he reaches for the door. "You're on," he says before he disappears inside, and I head up to the main deck to face the music. I imagine my mother won't be anywhere near as understanding as Aunty Joan, but the one thing I've learned from the women in my life is to not have any regrets. And I don't. I'm in love and I'm happy. I don't have any regrets at all.

NATE

"And here he is. The man of the hour." Joan shifts to the side a little so I can fit beside her on the couch. "Seems you've caused a bit of a stir."

"That wasn't my intention," I say as I sit. "I just wanted to help out a friend of a friend. Delaney and I met through Liz who is the little sister of my college roommate. Things escalated from there."

"I see. So, pretending to be the significant other of successful women isn't something you do on a regular basis?" I love how straight to the point this woman is. It's refreshing.

Chuckling slightly, I shake my head. "No. I've been a stand-in a few times, but it's a very rare occasion where I would escort a woman anywhere for a fee. There were...extenuating circumstances this time. And for what it's worth, I won't be taking any money now that we've become something more than just a job."

"I wouldn't have thought less of you if you did take the money. But I respect your decision. And your honesty. I hear your father passing away had a lot to do with your current situation. I'm sorry."

"Alcoholism. Was it Delaney who told you?" I ask, and she nods. "Did she explain what happened?"

"Just that things were tense between the two of you before he left us. It's not easy losing a loved one before you can reconcile."

Nodding slowly, I wonder for a moment if I want to explain exactly what happened between Dad and me. But I decide to let sleeping dogs lie. The chain of events that came after that moment is what led me right here to *this* moment. So I can't stay angry at him for that. If he hadn't damaged my career when he did, I may never have met the love of my life. In hindsight, he did me a favor.

"Let's just say everything changed after he passed," I say instead. "I felt the need to let go of my long-held dream and move my life in a different direction. Returning to San Francisco was the one thing that made sense. And now that I've met Delaney, I realize that's because my heart was there waiting for me to pretend to be her boyfriend."

Joan smiles. "I like that you called her your heart."

"Not just my heart, Joan. She's my soulmate. There's no doubt in my mind about it."

"You're making an old woman very happy talking like that, Nathaniel."

"Nate. Please."

"OK, Nate." She smiles as she searches my eyes for a moment. "There's something I'd like to give you. And you can refuse, but it would make *my* heart very happy to see it put to good use."

"OK."

She digs through her bag, her entire arm disappearing like she's Mary Poppins going through her carpetbag attempting to retrieve a lamp. It's quite comical to watch, even more so when her head disappears and her voice muffles.

"Ah, here it is," she says, straightening up and opening her hand before she meets my eyes with joy and distant memories held in hers. "This has been my most treasured item for many years, and now, seeing the way you are with my great-niece means I'd like to bequeath it to you. Perhaps it will do for you what it couldn't do for me."

"Couldn't do?" I look from her open hand to her eyes. "I'm sensing there's an interesting story behind this."

"Of course." She smiles at the memory as she gazes at the item and holds it up to the light. "There's a little more to my story than the family knows. And if you have some time, I'd like to tell it to you. And maybe when I'm finished, we'll all be working toward a new dream."

I turn my body toward her, taking her cool hand in mine as I smile. "You have my full attention, Joan."

She smiles, her gaze getting far away as she visits a distant memory. "It all started before the war…"

~

Delaney returns about twenty minutes after Joan has left. Her shoulders sag, and her nerves seem frayed. "Remind me never to lie to my mother again," she says as she flops on the bed beside me and groans into her pillow.

Smiling, I set the book she bought me aside and curl around her instead, my hand drifting up and down her spine in comfort. "I'm guessing it didn't go so great." I press a kiss to her shoulder.

"She made it all about her. And I ended up getting really snappy." She turns her face so she's looking into my eyes. Hers are a little bloodshot from frustration and tears.

I run my fingers through her thick hair,

brushing it away from her face. "Did you give her a piece of your mind?"

"I did, actually." She rolls to her side, and we entwine our fingers. "I told her she hurt me. That she always made me believe I wasn't good enough or pretty enough. She said she didn't believe that was true. And then I told her it was true, and that a mother is supposed to go out of her way to make her daughter feel worthy of love. But instead she acted like I was pitiful and undesirable unless the man was half blind."

"I hope you know that none of that is true. It never was."

"I do now," she says, turning her face to look into my eyes. "And I know I struggled to believe it in the beginning, but I do believe it now. Just the fact a man as gorgeous as you keeps tearing my clothes off has to mean something, right?" She smiles, and I shuffle closer to press a gentle kiss to her lips.

"I've got nothing to do with it, gorgeous. You were born beautiful, and you should have spent your life believing that. I want you to promise me that you won't allow your self-worth to be defined by what another human thinks of you. You are beautiful inside and out, and nothing on this earth can change that fact. Believe it. Own it. And tell anyone who says different to fuck off."

She places a hand on the side of my face as her

eyes glisten with unshed tears. "Gosh, I'm so ridiculously in love with you, Nate."

"Me too," I say, leaning in closer to kiss slow and long. "If memory serves me correctly, you wanted to spend the rest of the night lying in bed with absent clothes." I waggle my eyebrows.

"Absent clothes," she repeats with a laugh. "Yes, that's exactly what I need."

"The perfect Christmas Eve. I love you, gorgeous," I murmur before I kiss her like I mean it, pulling the zipper open on her dress so we can make good on that naked promise. And as the evening whiles away, I know that despite the drama at dinner, this night will be remembered fondly. Because it's the night we came out to the world as the people we are, the *couple* we are. It's only happiness from here. Especially since come Christmas morning, I have a *very* special surprise planned for my beautiful red-headed love.

DELANEY

*I*s it silly that at thirty-six I still feel the magic and wonder of waking up on Christmas morning? Like, somehow, Santa will have come down the chimney and filled my stocking, eaten the cookies, and drunk the milk.

Of course, I've been aware of the truth behind gift-giving since Mary Trunchberg ruined it all for me in the third grade. But besides that one wobbly year when I came to terms with things, I've always felt that childish excitement of waking up on December 25th and knowing it's a special day.

As I've gotten older, I've understood why Aunty Joan always insisted on hosting us at her house. Christmas just isn't Christmas without family and children to keep that wonder alive and well. As we grew and my brothers got married and started having kids of their own, I've really appreciated spending holidays as one big dysfunctional family, just for that moment on Christmas morning when the kids yell, 'Santa was here' then tear into their gifts.

But this year, I'm filled with wonder of a different kind. Because when I open my eyes on Christmas morning, my body achingly sated from yet another night filled with love-making, I'm presented with something I never in my wildest dreams imagined—Nate, wearing a Santa hat and *nothing else* as he kneels beside the bed on only one knee, a *heart-shaped diamond ring* pinched between two fingers.

"What is going on?" I gasp, my eyes wide as I drink him in.

The most delicious smile I've ever seen in my life spreads across his face. "Merry Christmas, gorgeous," he says as he moves the ring from side to side so the diamond catches the light. "I was kinda hoping you'd grant me a Christmas miracle by doing me the honor of becoming my wife."

"Kinda hoping?" Tears fill my eyes as I skooch to the side of the bed so I'm sitting and he's looking up at me with honest love and devotion in his beautiful blues.

"Desperately wishing," he says, taking my left hand in his. "I don't have a huge amount to give you, Delaney. But I do have my heart. I have my loyalty, my love, my admiration, and my intentions. Before I met you that day in the coffee house, I was lost, so incredibly lost and searching. But then I looked into your eyes and everything in the world seemed right again. Bam. Just like that. I can't see any way forward that doesn't involve having you by my side as my partner, my lover, my wife. It would make me beyond happy if you'd agree to spend your life with me. Will you marry me, Delaney?"

"Yes," I whisper, not even having to give it an extra moment of thought as my eyes fill with tears and Nate is sliding the ring on my finger before kissing my palm and gathering me in his arms. "I love you so much."

"I love you more," he says, holding himself over me and smiling brighter than I've ever seen. "You've made me the happiest man on the planet, gorgeous. And I'm going to spend the rest of my life making you the happiest woman in the universe. You are my heart and my soul, and I'm so fucking in love with you."

He brings his mouth down on mine, our tongues tangling and sliding as we roll until he's on his back and I'm straddled on top of him, taking him inside me as his magic fingers tease me exactly where he knows I like it. I moan and writhe, loving this deep and thorough connection we share, adoring the weight of the diamond on my finger, and admiring the way the light hits it as I rake my fingers over his chest as I come. *What a wonderful Christmas morning indeed.*

When we're lying tangled up together, and I'm holding my hand up above us, just staring at this new piece of bling that's adorning my ring finger, I feel so wonderfully complete I can barely stand it. "Did you have this with you the whole time?" I ask as I turn to meet his eyes and notice something flit across them, like a piece of information he's not sure he should be telling me. "Oh, don't tell me it was hidden inside that fleshlight. Because, eww."

He chuckles as he winds his fingers between mine then brings my hand to his lips and plants a kiss right next to the ring. "That's definitely not where it was hiding," he starts as he plays with the pink colored diamond with his forefinger and thumb. "This was actually hiding in the bottom of your aunt's bag. She told me that she's been carrying it around for seventy-five years."

"Really?" I had no idea.

Nate nods. "There was an English pilot she met during the final months of the war. Donald, his name was. He was on leave, and they fell in love, got engaged, and then he had to return to duty."

"Oh, no. Did he die? That's horrible. So close to the end."

"He didn't die in the war," he says. "When the war finished, he had to return to England and take over work in his family's company. Joan took over her father's candy store when he damaged his back taking a sugar delivery. Circumstances just kept getting in their way. He and Joan kept in contact for many years, but their timing was always off, their lives continually moving in different directions until one day...it was just too late. Donald passed away from a sudden heart attack, and Joan never ended up walking down the aisle to him like they planned. She gave this to me yesterday, hoping that we'd use it in the way she never got to, and that for us, it'd be a symbol of the hope and devotion she and Donald shared despite the distance between them."

My heart fills along with my eyes. "That's so tragically beautiful," I whisper, loving the ring even more now. "I never knew that about Aunty Joan, but everything makes so much more sense now. It wasn't about insisting I get married and pop out kids. It was about making sure I didn't miss my opportunity because I was too busy working to make a name for myself. I will treasure this always."

"And I'll treasure you," he murmurs, pressing a kiss to the tip of my nose. "Want to see what's in that sack beneath the tree?" He inclines his head toward it, and I sit up again and focus on it, almost forgetting it was even there.

"Do you already know?" I ask, wondering how much he and Aunty Joan have been conspiring together for my enjoyment.

"I don't. But I'm certainly curious. She said she gave the same thing to everyone."

"I hope it's matching ugly Christmas sweaters. That would be hilarious to wear during the festivities today. There's a big Santa party on the main deck for kids and a naughty Santa event for grownups. Our final day on the cruise is going to be a blast. Especially because I get to spend it with you, Nate. As an engaged woman no less."

"We could be in a hole in the ground, and I'd be happy," he says as he steps out of bed and picks up the sack from under the tree. "Seems too light to be sweaters." He rests it in front of me, and I look inside to find a glittery red box with green ribbon tied around it. It says, 'To Delaney & Nathaniel' which makes me smile because she either wrote this last night, or this is just because she knew all along.

"It feels empty," I say as I test its weight and give it a shake.

"Open it. Maybe she's pranking us all."

I grin, thinking that would actually be pretty funny. But when I pull the ribbon open and lift the lid, I find a very legal looking document with the heading: Gilchrist Family Trust.

"What on earth is this?" Reaching in, I unfold the papers, reading through the details. Seems Aunty Joan didn't like the idea of waiting until she dies to give to the people she cares about most in this world. So, she's set up a trust for each of us with a small fortune inside that will continue to give until long after she's gone. It brings tears to my eyes, of gratefulness and of longing, because this reminds me that my favorite aunt won't be with us forever. But mostly, it makes me feel very loved. My sweet aunt has thought of everything.

*

"I DIDN'T GET to have children of my own," Aunty Joan says as she makes a toast at dinner. "But my life has still been blessed with family, and so much joy. Having you all close, year after year has truly made me appreciate what a precious gift I've been given. That's why I've given you all access to your trusts now. I'm ninety-five years old. So I'd like to spend the remaining years of my life seeing you all *enjoy* life. And regardless of the dramatics we went through yesterday, I love each and every one of you equally. So this Christmas, my give to you is your inheritance. So, no stress over mortgages or who gets what"—she looks at

Tony for that one—"operating costs or business expansion"—that one is for me—"starting a new career"—that's for Nate—"or working jobs you hate to make ends meet." Those final words go to Tommy and my father. "Of course, I expect you to stay at my house every holiday the way we've always done. But I also expect that the weight of the world will be lifted off your shoulders, and your focus can be happiness instead of work or money. Believe me, in the end, it's the happy times that matter most. So cling to them, relish in them, enjoy them, and have a lifetime of Christmases that are just as good, if not better, than the one we've had this year."

"Here, here!" Dad says, lifting his glass as we all join in in chorus, thanking Aunty Joan for everything she's done in bringing us together, and keeping us together.

She is truly the heart of our family. Even when it felt like everything was falling apart only twenty-four hours ago, a few understanding words from her had us all pulling back together. Tony apologized for snooping in our cabin—not that it stopped both Nate and I giving him an earful, mind you—and Mom even apologized for setting me up with less than desirable men, then Dad apologized for not stepping in sooner. While a simple apology doesn't magically fix things, it did mean a lot to me to have that consideration given.

It means we're on the right path, and eventually, I hope all the pressure and the jealousy can be put behind us. Maybe this can be a new beginning for us all.

"Do you think we can talk?" Tony asks toward the end of the meal. I nod and follow him outside to stand on the balcony so we can talk in private. Nate makes it quite clear that if I need him, all I have to do is signal and he'll be beside me in a flash. "I need to apologize for what an asshole I was yesterday."

"Wow," I say, resting my forearms on the railing as I look out to the choppy sea. "Can't say I ever expected that. You never apologize."

"Christmas miracles and all that, right?" he says with a smirk as he slides his hands in his pockets and squints out at the horizon. "And the fact that my own children told me what a horrible person I was. They said I acted like the Grinch trying to destroy Christmas for everyone. Kind of made me stop and think, and realize that I was indeed an asshole for outing you like that. I should have just asked you straight up when I found the notepad lying on the floor in your room."

"That might have been a start," I say, as I pull my hair over my shoulder to stop it blowing about in the breeze. "I'll always love you, Tony. You're my big brother. But I admit that a lot of the time,

I don't understand you. It hurt me a lot, what you did yesterday. And in the spirit of Christmas, I can definitely forgive you for it. But it'll probably take me a while to trust you as a big brother again."

He nods slowly. "I deserve that. But thank you. I appreciate you always being the bigger person."

"I hope that wasn't a joke about my size," I tease, leveling him with my gaze as I offer him a smile too.

With a chuckle, he shakes his head. "Never, Del. You're perfect just the way you are. I think that's something we all should have been saying to you all along."

A lump forms in my throat as I nod then hold out my arms. "I think we need to hug this one out."

Grinning, he slides his arms around me and holds me tight. "I really am sorry, Del. I promise to be a better brother from here on out. And an awesome uncle too. We're all gonna be on your back about popping out babies now that you've landed the guy." He gestures toward my engagement ring as we end the embrace.

Laughing, I wipe the mistiness out of my eyes. "I'd expect nothing less."

"Everything OK?" Nate asks when we return, and I take my seat beside him again.

"Everything's absolutely perfect," I say, leaning in close and tilting my head up to view his gorgeous face. "This has turned out to be the most wonderful Christmas ever."

"It has, hasn't it?" he says, pressing his lips to mine and making me feel even more deliriously happy than I already was.

If there's one thing that came from Tony outing Nate and me the way he did, it's that I finally feel *seen* by everyone at this dinner table. All I ever wanted was the freedom to be myself and choose my own path. And I have, with Nate. We came together under messy circumstances and fell completely and hopelessly in love.

While I should probably feel bad about inventing Liam in the first place, I think I'm always going to be glad I did. Because without that fib, I never would have found my one, my heart, my true Christmas miracle. From here on out, I know that I'll be living the life I've always wanted, without regrets, without pressure, without fear. Because Nate is mine, and it's not just for the holidays, but for always.

EPILOGUE
NATE

Five years later...

"Are we sure about this?" I say as I clip the baby seat into the car. Our youngest, Suki, is fast asleep, her rosebud lips moving like she's drinking and her little fists balled up at her sides. She's like a tiny little doll, and my heart melts just looking at her.

"Of course!" Delaney says as she opens the opposite door and helps our three-year-old, Callum, into his booster seat. "She will love it. I promise you."

"If you say so."

Delaney smirks. "Are you doubting me, Nathaniel Charmers?"

"Never," I atone.

"Remember those hand care products you thought were too girly for men? Those have turned out to be some of our best sellers."

"For the record, I said they *smelled* girly. Not that men wouldn't like them."

"Whatever makes you sleep better at night, buddy," she teases as she finishes getting Callum clipped in then shuts the car door.

I straighten up and look at her over the top of our car. "You're never going to let me live that down, are you?"

With both kids clipped in safely for the journey, she rests her forearms on the roof, grinning a cheesy grin. "Never. I love it when I'm right. Like how teaching drama at community college has been super rewarding for you."

"I know, I know. Delaney knows best."

"Yes she does," she says, beaming as we slide into the front of the car and meet in the middle for a soft kiss.

"Have I told you how much I love you today?" I murmur, my heart still thundering whenever I so much as get near her. She is quite certainly the reason my blood continues to pump in my veins. I never understood what it was to be alive until I met her that day in the coffee house. Since then, my path became clear, and I have walked sure and true, hand in hand with my love. And if it's at all possible, I've fallen further and deeper for her in the meantime.

"You have. But I always want to hear it."

"I love you, Delaney."

"I love you, too."

Most guys I know say that the best part of being married is the lead up to the wedding. But for me, getting married was just the start. After a somewhat tumultuous beginning, Delaney and I settled into married life at what we thought would be the height of our love for each other. But then we just kept living at that height, feeling obsessed with each other, possessed by the need to be together. And my love grew. Then she fell pregnant with our first and my heart expanded to fit more in, then more, and more, until I realized that when you've found your soulmate, your ability to love is infinite. The point of being together is because you're a completion of each other, a complement to each other. So of course it works, because you belong.

"Are you ready to go?" Delaney says, buckling herself in. "We've not got long until our tiniest munchkin wakes up and wants food. I'm hoping we'll be there before that happens so I'm not feeding roadside."

"In that case," I say, starting up the car. "It's Oakwood Falls, here we come!"

DELANEY

A very muscular young man named Sven takes the keys and offers to park our car when we arrive at Aunty Joan's estate. "He's new," Nate says, as we collect the kids and our overnight bags then head inside.

I giggle as I watch him drive to the garages in our car. "She does enjoy collecting," I muse, loving that Aunty Joan actually did what she said she would and replaced her entire staff with muscular men. Some are ex-strippers, some are models, but all of them are candy for the sweet lady, and I swear that's how she stays so young.

"Happy 100th birthday, Aunty Joan!" I sing-song when we get inside and find her sitting in the entry hall speaking with Tony and Lucy about the size of the guest list. Seems the muscular man she charged with party preparations went through every telephone and address book she's ever kept and invited them all. And after 100 years on this earth, there are a lot of people Aunty Joan has connected with. So it's quite a turn out.

"I thought this was supposed to be a surprise party?" Nate says as we say quick hellos to Tony, Lucy, and their now-teenaged kids. Despite our early issues with Tony, we've come to hold each other in higher regard in the years since. He's apologized many times for snooping the way he did, and by now we've definitely forgiven him. "What are you doing sitting in the entry hall like a queen receiving her people?" That last part is directed to Aunty Joan as he presses a kiss to her rouge-covered cheek.

"Oh, it was supposed to be a big surprise," she says. "But I'm not so old that my brain quit working. I figured it out when Tommy asked where I keep my address book. I mean, honestly, what other reason could the man have for wanting it in the year I hit the century. One and one equals two and all that." She nods her head proudly, always loving that no one has ever been able to pull the wool over her eyes on anything.

"Sharp as a tack, Aunty Joan," I say as I press a kiss to her other cheek. Callum gives her a vigorous hug, and Suki just sleeps. But she'll be awake and wanting food before long. "Tonight is going to be spectacular. I just know it."

"Oh, of course. I'm getting some of these housemen to do a dance for us. PG of course, don't want to damage the children." She cackles and holds out her hand, a brunette man, who I think is called Roy, quickly comes to her aid and helps her into the next room where I can hear more chatter from guests. "Come and get something to drink. It's a party."

"We'll just drop our things off in our room and feed the baby, then we'll be down," I say, accepting the offer when Lucy offers to watch Callum for us so he can go and see Tommy and Tarryn and their kids who are still ten and eight, so a bit more fun for a three-year-old boy to play with.

"Looks like we're in for a big night," Nate says as he hoists the baby carrier onto the big bed.

"Well, Aunty Joan never does things by halves," I say as I coo at Suki and lift her from her carrier for a feed before I change her. Oh, have I mentioned how *gorgeous* Nate is when looking after our children? I've never seen a man who dotes on his kids the way my man does. Somehow, just seeing such a huge, strong man be so incredibly gentle with a tiny human just turns me into a big puddle of mush. If I wasn't already head over heels for him at the get-go, this fatherhood stuff would have been the clincher. He's a dream, and I'm so proud of the person he's become.

When we finished up our Christmas cruise, we spent the time between Christmas and New Year holed up together, just taking some one on one time. It gave him the chance to work out what he wanted to do next in life. Of course, we had our wedding to plan, but most important for Nate's peace of mind was finding somewhere to shift his professional focus. He didn't want to be a man of leisure, despite what the trust and my company could afford us and acting would always be a big part of who he is. So, he turned to teaching.

At first, he wasn't too sure how much he'd enjoy it. But once he had the chance to mentor and share his own love for the arts with others, he realized it was exactly what he'd been looking for.

Every facet of our lives seemed complete. We had each other, our careers, and it wasn't long until our own little family came along to add to our joy. And now, five years later, life is good. It's great, in fact. In each other, we have everything we'd ever want.

There hasn't been a moment over the last five years where I've had a moment of regret over how we started or how far we've come. Nate and I connected from the start, and we'll continue to be connected, completing each other from now until the day we take our last breaths, filled with years and years of happy memories. Because as Aunty Joan says, that's all that really matters—the happy moments. And I'll be forever grateful to her for providing the catalyst that helped me to find my happiest of moments in meeting the love of my life. Nate might have started out as a Band-Aid to fix a problem, but he very quickly became the salve that healed all of my wounds. With him by my side, there's nothing we can't do. He completes me. He's mine. And I am his. For always.

The End

NEXT FROM MEGAN: Christmas is coming with The Not So Silent Night, book one in the collaborative 'Santa's Coming' series.

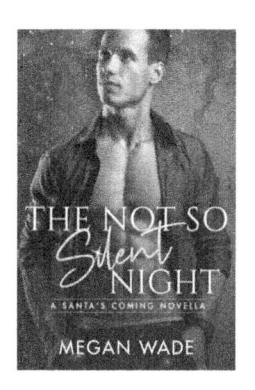

To discover more quick and dirty insta-love reads by Megan Wade. Sign up for her newsletter: https://www.subscribepage.com/meganwade

Follow her on Facebook: https://www.facebook.com/meganwadeauthor/

Join her Sweeties group: https://www.facebook.com/groups/959211654464973

Follow her in Instagram: https://www.instagram.com/meganwadewrites/

ALSO BY MEGAN WADE

Novels

Mine for the Holidays

Happy Curves Series

Sheets & Giggles

Sweet Curves Series

Marshmallow

Pumpkin

Pop

Sugarplum

Cookie

Sucker

Taffy

Toffee Apple

Peaches & Cream

Royal Curves Series

Rowdy Prince

Naughty Prince

Cheeky Prince

Wedded Curves Series

Whoa! I married a Mountain Man!

Whoa! I married a Billionaire!

Whoa! I married the Pitcher!

Whoa! I Married a Rock Star!

Whoa! I Married a Biker!

Collaborations

Boss Daddy (DILF for Father's Day)

Hayden's Firecracker (Holiday Firecrackers)

Chiseled Chest (Makes My Heart Race)

Her Cowboy Hero (American Heroes)

Cillian (The Kelly Brothers)

Break My Fall (Love Trap)

Tricks in the Night (Hot Halloween Nights)

Trick or Snowstorm (Tiaras & Treats)

The Not So Silent Night (Santa's Coming)

Made in the USA
Monee, IL
16 December 2020